Enchanted
BY THE
HIGHLANDER

A Time Travel Scottish Medieval

Romance: The Charmstones of Yore Book One

KM BOOKS

Kalani Madden

It cannot be stressed enough that this is a work of fiction, lovingly written around some interesting historical artifacts inherited by our modern-day culture. For all you genealogists and Campbell descendants out there, please enjoy this romanticized, fantastical tale with our grateful thanks to your illustrious ancestors for providing such excellent romantic material.

Black Colin Campbell is a real historical figure. He is remembered in history as the Third Earl of Argyll, First Laird of Glenorchy, Laird of Ardkinglas, Lochgoilhead, and Argyllshire. His birth is estimated to have been anywhere between 1396 and 1400 CE; the year of his death is more precise, given in one book as September 14, 1475. During his long life, he was married four times, with his first wife being Mariott (her name was also recorded in their marriage dispensation as Marion) Stewart, with whom he had no children before her passing.

Please note that for the purposes of this narrative, Sir Colin (and his wife) has been made a composite of several medieval-era Colin Campbells alive during 1300 - 1475 CE. The name of Colin Campbell has long been associated with Kilchurn Castle as they all lived close to the shores of Loch Awe.

The Campbell Charmstone is also real. Owned by the Campbells of Glenorchy in Argyllshire, the ancient crystal has been dated back to the Dark Ages, at the beginning of the seventh century (600 CE). One side of the crystal is indeed damaged. Legend has it that Black Col wore the charmstone when he fought the Turks in Rhodes, Southern Greece, in the mid-15th century. Black Colin Campbell is buried at Kilmartin Church Cemetery, Argyll and Bute, in Scotland.

In later life, Black Colin's sobriquet was changed to 'Gray Colin,' after his black hair faded white. It is not known whether the name referred to his temperament or his hair.

Contents

Prologue   *5*

Chapter 1   *11*

Chapter 2   *17*

Chapter 3   *25*

Chapter 4   *33*

Chapter 5   *43*

Chapter 6   *53*

Chapter 7   *63*

Chapter 8   *73*

Chapter 9   *83*

Chapter 10   *91*

FREE - Black Colin & the Lady of Loch Awe   *99*

Prologue

Black Col Campbell, Knight of Loch Awe, hid amidst the ruins, waiting for the Saracens to plod past on their caravan of camels. They were many leagues from the boat left docked on the side of the Euphrates River and their guide had abandoned them.

The ancient structure's remains dotted the dry landscape all around him; the crumbling pillars poked out of the sand like spillikins waiting for a ball to send them tottering over. This is where Sir Colin Campbell and his band of soldiers had decided was the best place to lie and wait for the road to clear of domestic travelers, those whose allegiances might not be the same as the Scottish Highlanders hidden from sight amidst the dunes.

It was meant to be the last war fought at the behest of the Church. The Pope in Rome had asked for all Catholic men to come to the aid of Eastern Orthodoxy. Once again, Constantinople was under attack, this time from Mehmed II. The empire was exhausted after its population had been cut in half by the Black Death; its defenses had shrunk to a few miles short of the city of Constantinople itself.

If Mehmed won, the Ottoman Empire would fall, taking the teachings of Christ with it.

He cast his mind back to his sweet wife's words to him before he set out:

"This might be our final parting, Husband. What will ye have me do if this is so?"

Black Colin had focused on tightening the stirrup straps so his wife would not see the emotion in his face. "If that happens, Marriott, I command ye to be happy and remarry as ye will't."

She had laughed, a wild sounding cascade of mirth. "I have seen over twenty summers come an' go, Husband. If this is our final farewell, I vow to remain chaste so that I can still stand as your wife in heaven."

Sweeping her into his arms, he had growled into her ear so that none but she could hear it. "I will move heaven and earth to come back to ye, sweetheart. This I vow upon our love."

Those words were of some comfort to Sir Colin as he lay hunkered down in the sand.

Looming in the distance was a struggling forest of hardy pines refusing to die on top of shale and rock. When he looked to the west, Col could see tiny crystal shards of soil sparkling under the light of the moon. Black Col's guide had told him the ruins had once been devoted to the worship of an ancient Greek deity, but all signs of the priests and temple maidens had long since gone, leaving only broken statues behind. The pedestal behind which Col was hiding had one faded word etched on it: Κρόνος.

How he had grown to loathe the slipping sand that dominated this patch of pagan land. He hated the way it shifted under his feet and found its way into his mouth and in between his teeth. But most of all he distrusted how it would twist into furious dust devils when his back was turned, only to morph into a thunderstorm that darkened the sky moments later. He used the darkness to his advantage, and crouched down silently behind a great fallen statue, waiting for the track to empty so they could make their way back to the river.

His men were battle-hardened soldiers like himself: plain clansmen raised on the plain food of the Highlands. Their supplies of oatmeal had not even lasted long enough to get them to Rome. The palmer who had led them to the Pope to get his blessing for the small part they wanted to play in his Holy War had long departed, blithely telling them that he had seen the great temple of Sophia once and had no desire to see it again.

The rascal! Black Col now knew what it felt like to be a lamb led to slaughter. How many times had he survived this mad escapade by the skin of his teeth, only to rue his noble but misguided actions at Glenorchy? What he wouldn't give to inhale the sweet smell of white heather on the misty island hills once more and hold his beloved Mariott in his arms.

Instead, swept away by the palmer's words, he had gripped the hilt of his dirk and sworn on the cross to obey the summons of Constantine XI.

The Hagia Sophia was not the magnificent temple on a golden hill he had imagined it to be: it was a war zone. A place where rabid

Turks, fanatical Saracens, and dread disease lurked around every corner and hid inside every latrine. At least it was nighttime now: being eaten by sand midges was better than being tortured by flies.

They will call me Black Col with a vengeance when I return to me bonny wife in the Highlands. Me temperament is soured from this barbaric land, and me skin is burnished as brown as the leaves before they fall off the tree branches.

Col Campbell mused to himself as he checked to see if the caravan had riders lagging behind.

His clan called him by the sobriquet Black Col because of his pitch black hair and sallow skin: traces left over from a Southern French bride in one of his forebears' pasts. It was an unusual physical attribute to have in a place so close to the Norse Lands, but Col was not complaining about his dark coloring now; he was the only one in his cadre of soldiers whose skin had not suffered under the harsh Turkish sun.

"Sir," one of his soldiers had crawled on his belly to speak quietly beside him, "we willna be able to cross this way. Let's find another path to leave by."

A small boy was walking a donkey along the road and swishing languidly at its hindquarters with a thin willow branch. Being so young, his hearing was acute. He heard the strange pattern of speech spoken in the dark, coming from Black Col's hiding place in the ruins.

Giving the donkey a furious cut with the stick, the boy tilted his head back and began ululating into the air. "Hulla-lul-lul-lul-lu-lu-lu!"

The shriek felt as if it was piercing Col's guts. All would be lost if they didn't run into the hills and hide behind the sharp stones that jutted between swaying pines.

Leading the way, with his soldiers following hard behind, Black Col made a mad dash for the sandy ridges that surrounded the ruins. Running on the sand was a nightmare. The dunes seemed to move further away instead of coming closer as his boots slipped on the grains. Their footsteps would leave an obvious trail even if they did make it to the trees in time.

Answering ululations could be heard coming from behind them, eventually joined by the thump of hooves on sand. Pursuit was afoot.

His breath rasping, his throat on fire, Col scrambled up a shallow dune, running on all fours like a beast of the field. If he had been dressed like a king's knight in full armor, he would never have made it, but he was the Knight of Loch Awe. His raiment consisted of narrow hose with a woolen plaid pleated around his waist and pinned over his chest: clothing light as air and warm as a freshly baked bannock. Spying a thin crack in the dune rocks, Col pushed inside it, never caring that the razor edged stone sliced at his skin as he did so.

He paused in the dark and stilled his ragged breathing, waiting for his men to follow behind him, but they never did. Pushing further back into the crevasse, Col watched for the moonlight streaming through the crack to alert him to pursuit. He was concerned about water - his waterskin would only last him three days at most - but he was not worried about someone following him inside. They would die before they reached him with his dirk between their ribs.

It was a perilous situation. Alone in the dark, Sir Colin smiled upon realizing that he was in the very definition of a tight spot. Pressing back into the crack in the rocks as far back as he could go, the Knight felt his breathing slow when they found him. The night sky and moonlight flickered as a shadow blocked out the stars.

The Saracens muttered amongst themselves and then placed their mouth at the entrance to speak into the crack. Col did not bother replying.

Let them wonder who I am. I might be a runaway prisoner, escaped from the same Barbarians and Infidels they slaughtered on the sands. If they dinnae ken who I am, then they cannae kill me.

The mutters became irate shouts and orders for Col to reveal himself, but all he did was press further back into the crack.

After a while, the shadows at the crevasse entrance disappeared and were replaced by peaceful starlight, but Col was not fooled. His patience was eventually rewarded when his pursuers returned.

More orders and shouts. Col remained resolutely silent, but he knew his doom was tapping him on the shoulder.

A snapping sound broke the still night, followed by two more heavy scratching thuds. Black Col, Knight of Loch Awe, knew that sound: his pursuers had thrown three bundles of kindling inside the crack in the rocks.

God save me beautiful wife, Marriot. She was a good and gentle woman. May she have loving memories o'me. God bless me clan. God save me soul...

Acrid smoke began to fill the slim crevasse. Colin Campbell fell to his knees, retching and coughing, but still praying.

If I were to pray for one last thing, it would be to see the sunrise o'er the lush green hills that surround me home...hear the cries o' seabirds as they wing their way back to the nest...Kilchurn Watchtower standing on the banks of the bonny Highland isle lochs...an' me sweet wife...

The flames were licking in front of his face and Col was seized with the mad urge to throw himself onto the pyre. But that would be a mortal sin. He must wait for the flames to come to him. Sobbing, he dug his hands into the sand and bent his head so that he would not have to watch the fire consume him.

It was as if the charmstone was waiting in the sand for him. Coughing so hard it felt like pieces of his chest were spewing out of him, Col could clearly see the egg-shaped stone in his hand as the sands sifted away through the gaps between his fingers. The crystal was a sullen, dun color; hard as nails, cold as ice. It did not reflect the flickering fire but seemed rather to absorb it.

As Colin's fingers tightened around the smooth, oval stone, he felt more powerful than he believed was possible. The blood oozing from the thin rock cuts in his skin dropped onto the stone but seemed to melt off the crystal's curve as if the stone was repelling the red humor.

I wish I was back home in Loch Awe.

And then suddenly, he was.

Chapter 1

"Please stop talking about the inheritance my gran left me," Ella closed her eyes as she said the words. Generally, she was a polite young woman, but no amount of wealth and interesting knick knacks would bring her comfort. "Possessions mean nothing to me, you realize."

The lawyer stopped talking and allowed Ella time to recover. It was difficult for Ella to swallow down the lump in her throat. Although she would never describe herself as an hysterical person, being left all alone in the world once again was hard to bear. After searching her pockets, Ella Campbell found the tissue she was looking for, and began using it to blow her nose and blot the tears from her eyes. The soft paper immediately disintegrated in her hand, leaving flakes of white tissue on the chair, desk, and her shirt.

"Tea or coffee?" Mr. McKaye quickly asked Ella as she began to brush the paper flakes off all the surfaces with brisk, agitated strokes. "Tea, please, thank you," Ella said in a distracted tone.

This being Glenorchy in New Zealand, there was no receptionist or intercom - such things were only to be found on the legal shows on television - Mr. McKaye got up to boil the kettle in the corner of his office, which he only worked from one day of the week. The bulk of his business came from farmers making livestock transactions and real estate deals to open ski resorts up in the looming Milford Sound mountains. And, of course, Neville McKaye made a good living writing up Health and Safety contracts for travelers coming for the never-ending Lord of the Rings tours that were still proving fruitful, even though filming had wrapped almost twenty years ago.

"I knew your gran all my life," Neville McKaye said, busy with the tea bags and mugs. "We all called her Nana Campbell as kids. Her tablet and shortbread were always a sellout at the church market fairs."

"I think I can find the recipe for you if you want," Ella wanted to make it up to the lawyer for her crotchets. "Hang on, if you want it, I can write it down for you now. I know most of Gran's recipes off by heart."

Returning to his desk, Neville placed the mug of tea next to Ella's elbow and then put the small tray with milk and sugar between them, before sitting down. "Mrs. McKaye might not be pleased if I come home with another woman's fudge recipe in my pocket," Neville replied, after giving Ella's offer some thought.

Ella liked her brew strong, milky, and sweet, and busied herself making the tea the way she wanted it, stirring the spoon around in the mug at a vigorous pace. When it was ready, she sat back in the chair and smiled. "'*The cup that cheers, but doth not inebriate.*' Gran taught me that quote a few months after I came to live with her - my parents were coffee drinkers."

Mr. McKaye smiled and nodded, but did not make eye contact. "Er...sorry, Ella, but you have tissue paper stuck to your face..."

"Fouter!" Ella muttered, searching through her bag for a hand mirror and after failing to find it, settled for rubbing her face with her hands. It didn't matter much; her mascara was ruined anyway.

"How's that?" she asked the lawyer, tilting her face toward him for a closer inspection.

"F-fine, fine," Neville McKaye stuttered. It was not often a young woman who looked like Ella Campbell leaned over his desk toward him.

She was an unusually beautiful girl, no more than nineteen years of age. The unusual part came from her silver-blonde waist-length hair and matching pale eyebrows. The beautiful part came from her pansy-colored eyes. They were arrestingly purple encircled with black, just like the dark purple pansies that chefs used to decorate salads: edible flowers, those decorative purple pansies were called nowadays. However, no flower could ever look as delightful as Ella Campbell's eyes. Her lashes were fair enough to allow the color of her eyes to blaze out at the observer without distraction; her eyelashes were the only part of her face with pigment, being a light brown color once the mascara washed off.

Ella's other features were normal in comparison to her eyes; a straight nose and a wide, generous mouth. The shape of her face was defined by the addition of slanting cheekbones, a small chin, and a white oval forehead, but a heart-shaped face embellished by eyes like that made sense to everyone who knew Ella. She was the epitome of someone whose eyes were the window to her soul.

At times, she could be misty and mauve; at other times, Ella would blaze black and violent violet. It all depended on her mercurial moods.

"What was that you said?" Neville wanted to know. "From the way you rolled the 'rrr' sound at the end, I would guess it was a Scottish word."

Ella had the grace to blush, but didn't mind explaining. "Fouter. It comes from the French word, 'foutre,' which is the French equivalent of the English eff word. In ancient times, the Scots took the French word and Scottified it up with the rolling 'r' sound you recognized. But now it means an irritating incident or bumbling person. My Gran used to say if I must swear, then I could use a good old Scots 'fouter'. It also lends itself to 'foutering' if you like. For example: *that foutering sports team of mine lost again*'."

Neville laughed and then remembered he was there to read the late Mrs. Isobel Campbell's will to her granddaughter. Sobering up, he put his solemn face back on.

"Very interesting, I'm sure. I know you don't want to dwell on it, Ella, but you are your Gran's heir. Just as you only had her, remember that she only had you too. It must bring you some comfort to know that you brightened your nana's last years. She loved you very much, you know. She even had me write it in her will." Neville tapped a sentence with his fingertip and began reading. "To my darling granddaughter who brightened my life from the moment she came to live with me, I leave all my worldly possessions."

Ella screwed up her eyes tightly as she listened, but she was determined not to dissolve into tears or tantrums again. She knew Granny Campbell would spin in her grave if she heard Ella being snippy with the lawyer.

Twelve years before, she had arrived to live with her gran, her father's mother, as a seven-year-old orphan. From what she could remember, her parents had been archetypal go-getters in their thirties, so upwardly mobile that they probably would have run out of aspirations by the time they reached fifty. It was as if her father, Gyllis Campbell, wanted to take his mother and father's plain life and increase everything about it tenfold.

Whereas gran had a small souvenir shop in Glenorchy, chock-full of what she was happy to call gewgaws and kitsch, Gyllis Campbell's small chain of high-end stores in Auckland had only stocked the best products. Melanie, Ella's mother, had mixed motherhood with running the chain's website. Most of what Ella could remember of her mother was a distracted 'mmm' whenever she had gone into Melanie's home office to play beside the desk.

And then they were gone. The babysitter had woken her up in the morning, telling her to get dressed and eat her breakfast like a good girl. It wasn't the first time Ella had spent the weekend at home with a babysitter looking after her, so she thought nothing strange about that. "Can you read me the message momma sent last night please, Aroha?"

Melanie would always send a voice message or video whenever Ella's parents went away for a romantic weekend together. This time it had been a luxury resort near Split Apple Rock in Tasman Bay.

"That I can't do, sweetheart," Aroha had said, shaking her head and walking to the sliding doors to look down the driveway. "Please eat your breakfast. Someone important is coming to visit."

Spooning the cereal into her mouth, Ella was excited. "Is it Hahona? Is he coming to play?" Hahona was Aroha's son, who went to the same school as Ella. Aroha didn't reply. Even twelve years later, Ella could remember the haunted expression on her babysitter's face as the woman stood with her forehead pressed against the sliding door glass, watching the driveway like a hawk.

Ella's memory was clouded and she struggled to remember Granny Campbell arriving to take her back to Glenorchy. Her parents had driven off one of the steeply descending South Island roads; one U-turn was all it took for Ella's life to bend around sharply too. Goodbye to the bustling metropolis of Auckland and hello to Glenorchy and its two pubs, one café, and half a dozen tourist trap shops. The nearest big city was Christchurch, but that wasn't saying much because most of the South Island spent a large portion of the year covered in snow and the rest of the year warding off gales blowing in from Antarctica and the occasional earthquake.

Unlike Ella's poor late mother, Melanie, Gran had all the time in the world for Ella. Every morning, Granny Campbell would wake her granddaughter up and tell her to shake a leg before her porridge cooled. Once she had graduated to grade nine, on weekdays Gran would take Ella to school in Queenstown, driving the lakeside route in her little green hatchback car. When the end-of-school bell sounded at three every afternoon, the little green hatchback would be waiting faithfully in the car park for Ella to climb in.

During the harsh South Island winters, Gran would have a flask of homemade soup in the backseat for Ella to sip with an ecstatic sigh as they began the homeward journey. In spring and summer, they might stop off at the long Lake Wakatipu to paddle and swim, and then the flask would be filled with vivid orange-flavored cool drink.

If Ella ever missed her parents, Gran would be there to comfort her, wrapping her in a warm embrace and patting Ella up and down her spine until the young girl's tears abated. "I miss momma," Ella would weep, the sobs making her shudder and hiccup no matter how much she told herself that all the crying in the world could never bring her parents back.

"There, there, lamb," Gran would croon, "they've gone to a better place."

Try as she might, Ella couldn't imagine her mom and dad sitting on a cloud in the sky, playing a golden harp. By the time she was eleven, she had stopped crying for her parents and decided that there were some gulfs too wide to bridge, death being one of them.

Neville McKaye's voice slowly came back into focus. "So, you're to inherit the shop - Isobel was canny enough to buy the land and the bricks-and-mortar structure with your grandfather's life insurance payout - and all the stock in the inventory."

A little smile lilted over Ella's mouth. All those fridge magnets with plastic Kiwis and Tui birds, all those Mount Cook Aoraki keyrings, and all those crystal snowballs that made white flakes fall on a tiny plastic mold of Glenorchy when it was shaken; they belonged to her now.

As a seven-year-old, the Campbell gift shop had been a treasure trove of wonders for her, but the wonder had faded over time after Ella discovered that the mesmerizing icons were nothing more than cheap, badly painted polyresin, mass-produced items, Made in China stickers on the bottom of these authentic 'New Zealand' souvenirs.

"You're going to have to find someone to run the shop for you, Ella if you don't want to do it yourself. Mrs. Biggins is too elderly to work there forever."

Mrs. Biggins was one of Gran Campbell's oldest friends in both senses of the word: Abby Biggins had been Isobel's governess on the family farm over seventy years ago when Gran Campbell had been a small child.

"She must be ninety if she's a day. I know." Ella shook her head, hoping that Neville McKaye understood the pickle she had been in after Gran died so suddenly. One moment Isobel Campbell had been preparing tea in the kitchen, and the next moment she was lying on the linoleum floor, her eyes staring up at the ceiling, unfocused and blank.

Feeling the lump pressing back into her throat, Ella quickly began to talk. "Abby did volunteer to fill in until I got my ducks in a row," she explained, "but I've had an offer from Pania, my cousin. She says she can take over running the shop for me - on one condition."

Gran Campbell's brother, Colin, had passed away two years previously. He had never officially married his de facto wife, Marama, and the legacy all Campbell siblings inherited from their parents was to make sure to pass down the family heirlooms to those with a Campbell clan surname.

"Pania is Marama and your Great Uncle's youngest daughter, isn't she?" Neville said after recollecting the fairly complicated Glenorchy Campbell family tree.

"Yes. Marama and Colin's other kids are all grown up, and they want to continue working on Campbell Farm because it's their mom's: Pania is the exception. She wants a life outside of the shadow of the mountains. I suppose working at the gift shop is a good place to start. At least she'll be closer to the bus stop there…"

"So, what is the condition Pania has asked for?"

Ella gave a wistful smile. "She will work at the shop full time, and keep all of the profits to tide her over any lean times…but she wants to live in Gran Campbell's cottage…alone."

Chapter 2

Neville McKaye sat back in his creaky desk chair, steepling his fingers in front of his mouth. "Where will you live, Ella?" he wanted to know. "In one of the holiday rentals?" He knew the trust fund Ella had inherited from her parents would keep her comfortable for a long time: money was not the issue here. It was unusual for a young woman in the last year of her teenage life to be left with just a few of her great-uncle's offspring as kin.

"I'm going on holiday myself, Neville, but I won't need a Glenorchy rental house to do it...at least not *this* Glenorchy." Mr. McKaye was the first person Ella was going to tell. She hadn't breathed a word about her plans before this. If the events in her life had taught Ella anything, it was to never plan too far ahead. "I'm leaving. I want to visit the land of my forefathers, Scotland."

Someone who wanted to leave was not a shocking revelation for anyone in Glenorchy to hear, especially when young folks were involved. There was a certain measured pace of life in the small village, as if the region's metronome was set to sway to a different beat. Spring would crawl into bloom once the winter snows melted; summer would warm the chilled earth, if only to make the grass green and the lake blue. And then the leaves seemed to remember with a lazy flutter to turn brown and fall, just enough to allow the slow cycle to start all over again. Time didn't fly in Glenorchy: it shuffled.

"I haven't decided where I will end up: maybe I'll backpack around Europe for a bit," Ella lied, "but please could you draw up a contract for me and Pania? And don't forget to deduct your fees from the trust fund once the bank has approved the paperwork."

Neville McKaye told Ella not to worry, he would handle the rental agreement for her Gran's old cottage, but could he perhaps add a date for when the contract would be renewed or voided? In that way, Ella would be able to take over the running of the gift shop and move back into her Gran's cottage when she returned.

"Sure, Mr. McKaye. Please do that. If Pania wants to continue running the shop and staying at the cottage while I'm away, her request should take precedence. And please arrange with the trust for them to pay the storage facility every month."

"Storage facility? Oh my…" Neville McKaye looked alarmed. "How long are you planning to be away, Ella!?"

Giving a rueful grin as she stood up, Ella moved to the door before the lawyer could dart around to the front of his desk to shake her hand goodbye. "Pania doesn't want all my books in the cottage when she lives there - and I'm sure I don't blame her! Cheers Neville, and thank you for everything."

***

Even though Campbell Cottage wasn't made from wattle and daub or had a thatched roof made of straw, the structure resembled a cottage on most points, including the chimney built from local rocks for the stone hearth on the east-facing side of the house. There was a climbing rose-laden archway above the white picket fence gateway entrance, and a moss-covered stone path leading up to the front door. The windows were paned too.

Like most New Zealand houses, the cottage had been constructed from the slow-growing pine wood lumber cut from the surrounding forests. But in a country where Victorian-era houses were deemed to be of huge cultural and historical significance, any building over one hundred years old was happily described as venerable.

This is where Ella had called her home for over a decade. Pushing open the front door, a blast of old book smell heated by the warm summer air overwhelmed her senses. Not all of the old books were hers; more than two-thirds of them had belonged to Gran Campbell. Even since she had come into her trust fund nine months ago, Ella had done two things: obtained a computer-chipped passport and begun to collect even more old books.

First Edition C. S. Evans' Sleeping Beauty, illustrated by Arthur Rackham; First Edition Lord of the Rings (of course) and The Hobbit; First Edition Mervyn Peake's Gormenghast trilogy, with Steerpike and Fuchsia gloomily staring at her from the steel plate engraving prints inserted into the page folds. These books were her treasures, beloved objects past price.

Gran Campbell had read to Ella from a precious old book every night of her childhood.

Ella would lie in bed with the Antarctic winds screeching around the cottage walls, listening to her Granny reading The Legend of Brigadoon, and Sir Walter Scott's Waverley novels and Ivanhoe. Maybe some adults grew up with R. D. Blackmore's Lorna Doone or Robert Louis Stevenson's Treasure Island echoing in their ears as they fell asleep, but Ella had always insisted that her bedtime books contain fairy tales or witchcraft, which Granny had been happy to oblige - just so long as the books involved the country of her grandparents' birth: Scotland.

Ella knew everything there was to know about the Wulver, the Selkies, the Bean Nighe, the Blue Men of Minch, and Kelpies.

Once, Ella asked her gran why she ran a gift shop when a bookstore devoted to ancient tomes and moth-eaten publications with yellow parchment pages that smelt of must and dust would have been so much more appropriate. Gran had replied: 'Because I never want to associate books and reading with work; they are far better as a pleasurable pastime.'

Now back in the cottage, Ella addressed her library. "I'm sorry, old friends," she spoke to the lines of books squeezed tightly into the bookcase shelves, "but it's the storage facility for you. Yes, Mrs. Beeton, I'm talking to you too. Pania gets her recipes off the internet, so it's the box for you."

Ella chatted to her books the way other folks spoke to their children or pets: in a conversational way that had nothing to do with expecting an answer back. "But fear not, my darlings, because I plan on doing the packing myself. The next time we meet, you will stink of naphthalene balls and be covered in pinewood shavings."

The rest of the day was spent with the tedious task of forming boxes and taping them in such a way that would prevent the books from falling out the moment someone picked the box up. Dozens and dozens of small boxes were required because large boxes of books would be too heavy to lift. Soon, there was no space in the parlor left to stand.

Gran Campbell had always called the small room on the left of the passage when someone entered the cottage, the 'parlor.' Ella was reprimanded whenever she called her gran to tell her a visitor was in the living room. "Parlor or drawing room is the correct term, Ella dear," Granny would say in her gentle way. "It's where we receive guests."

As a child, Ella thought it was called a parlor because there was no television for visitors to watch at Gran's house, unlike the massive flat screen that had dominated her parents' living room back in Auckland. She was soon to learn that there was no television in Campbell Cottage at all, and never would be - it was books or nothing. This might have been considered to be a Spartan existence by anyone who didn't know Isobel Campbell better, and Ella soon grew used to it and sometimes even enjoyed the peace.

Isobel Campbell's great-grandparents had grown up in nineteenth Glasgow, which had been no picnic. Even though the Campbells had left on a ship for New Zealand at the first opportunity they got, they brought their staunch post-Calvinistic beliefs with them. Porridge was flavored with salt, not sugar; frolicking was frowned upon; children were to be seen and not heard. This regimen had been passed on to subsequent generations.

Luckily for the orphaned Ella, the only thing gran had kept from her parents' rigid upbringing was their mistrust of television. Other than that, Ella had an idyllic childhood once she had settled in Glenorchy.

Packing up a library's worth of books took far longer than expected. Switching off the light, Ella promised the remaining books on the shelves that she would continue boxing them up tomorrow. "Enjoy your freedom while it lasts," she whispered to the books before shutting the door, "only one day of sunlight left." This was her own personal joke because no Campbell book was permitted to see the sunlight in case it damaged the parchment or faded the print.

Returning to the cramped space of her bedroom with a bowl of cereal to eat for supper, Ella settled down to read a book that had caught her eye while she was packing.

"'The Breadalbane Muniments associated with the Black Book of Taymouth: Their Relation to Highland Heroes, Myths, & Legends," Ella mused out loud, turning the hard leather-covered volume around to see the date of publication on the back: 1705. The blurred block print inside the old book testified to the book's age. Wriggling back into the soft pillows until she was comfortable, Ella began to read.

'*Dispensation for marriage, Laird Col. Campbell and Mariott Stewart, who have been living together in the state of fornication-*' Ella broke off her reading to add commentary to the words. "Ooh, Laird Col.

You dirty old man, you! But I bet the church was making a mountain out of a molehill." She continued reading because anything to do with the Campbell clan interested her, and Gran must have obtained or kept the book for a reason. '*-ignorant of the fact that they are related in the second, third, and fourth degrees of affinity and consanguinity.*'

Ella found it interesting enough and decided to give the book a few more pages, but if it didn't move from boring fact to enchanting history by then, she would be more than happy to place the book back in the box and tape the lids shut.

She already knew that consanguinity was a ploy the church used against the wealthy and elite Scottish nobles to squeeze money out of them: because clan chieftains and ladies intermarried amongst themselves to broaden their influence and add to their coffers, everyone was related after a generation or two. That was when the church stepped in to say that cousins connected by any degree on the family tree were not allowed to marry without obtaining a special (expensive) dispensation to wed from the clergy first.

What was unusual was that Col and Mariott had lived together openly before their marriage - there had to be an interesting story related to that fact somewhere!

'*And thus did a happy union betwixt man and wife begin, but the true start of the Campbell family saga stretches back even further, all the way back to the 13th century. In the Great Scottish verse-chronicle poem, 'The Brus,' it is recounted in Early Scots language, from the lips of Blind Harry Bard himself, that the rise of the Campbell clan began when then first Sir Colin was fortunate enough to have Mary (sister to Robert the Bruce) as his stepmother. By all accounts, Colin was a winsome child and much beloved by his stepmother. However, this close kinship was not necessary to put Colin on the road to renown: he was a second cousin once removed to Robert the Bruce on his great-great-grandfather's side (and cousin to W. Wallace).*

Thus, we can trace this earliest member of the Campbell clan and patriarch to the Earls of Argyll and the Locale Argyle, back to William Wallace and King Robert I during the mid-twelfth century.

He was known by many names: Sir Colin Og Campbell of Loch Awe; Cailean Óg Caimbuel; Colyn Cambel; Coline Oig Campbell. It is prudent to note that these names might have been passed on to Campbell sons, and did not belong to one or the same person; the difference in names comes from that juncture in history when the Scots language was defining itself away from Irish Gaelic.'

Ella was strangely comforted by the words in the book. "*You* have a date with my travel bag, Book. If I'm going to Scotland, I may as well take you with me." After carefully wrapping the book in a soft chamois leather cloth, she put it in a Ziploc bag previously used for sandwiches. Then the book was lovingly placed in the waterproof section of her backpack. Like all teens of her generation, Ella wouldn't be caught dead traveling with a hard-shell suitcase.

After cleaning her teeth in the bathroom she had shared with her Gran for most of her life, Ella fell asleep: she had a monumental day ahead of her. That night, she dreamed of an army of ancient Scottish lairds marching toward her across the universe of time and space, but that was a normal occurrence for Ella and one that she had no problem telling herself came from reading old books about the Campbell clan at bedtime.

It was backbreaking work the next day, packing all the books into the boxes. The removal van arrived before she had finished. Ella felt embarrassed as the driver and his helper offered to assist her after staring at the dozens of still unpacked books lying on every surface in the room.

"Fond of reading, are you?" the driver asked Ella. He was drinking tea while his helper packed the books. Busy cutting off tape with her teeth and handing it to the helper, Ella said "Uh-huh."

"I listen to this amazing podcast while I'm driving," the driver told her in a cheerful voice after dunking a biscuit and swallowing it down. "It's about Ancient Greek mythology. It's totally crazy what those people got up to and what they believed."

"Not much has changed then," Ella grinned, passing another box to the helper. She listened politely as the driver waffled on about Greek Gods and Greek heroes, before coming to a decision. "I have an early edition of Robert Graves' Greek Myths, Volumes One and Two here. If you like, you can have it." The book was worth far more than what the removal driver was charging her to deliver the books to the Queenstown storage facility, but Ella didn't say that: she was just happy that someone seemed to like myths and fables as much as she did.

"Thank you, Ella, but no," the driver shook his head, "I can see you love your books, and if you gave a couple to me they would end up in a cupboard in the house somewhere. It's a podcast or audiobook for me, I'm afraid, what with all the driving I do."

Ella understood. Books were a commitment. They were heavy and took up space. They required dusting, insect repellant, and shade; somewhere to stand when the reader was finished with them, and somewhere to lie while they were being read. They were easy to lose, steal, or be 'borrowed' by someone who would never bring it back. Books could be heartbreaking and satisfying at the same time. How much power did a book have to be able to make someone weep uncontrollably, while they were dying to know what the next page would bring at the same time? If a man did that to her, she would leave him in a heartbeat. She loved books for that reason alone.

"Would you like another biscuit?" she said, handing the tape to the sweating helper.

Two hours later, all the Campbell Cottage books were gone. Ella went to her bedroom to have one last cry. It was the end of an era and definitively the end of her childhood.

It was evening by the time she raised her face off the pillow and looked around the little bedroom. Sighing and feeling slightly sick from eating too many biscuits with the removal van driver, Ella went to Gran Campbell's bedroom to fetch her jewelry box. There was the amulet charmstone attached by the suspension loop to the leather thong. Gran had insisted the amulet stay on the thong, and refused to buy a silver chain to match the stone's mounting.

Ella wrinkled her nose as she touched the leather thong. It was black with age and greasy from countless fingers fingering it and who knew how many dirty necks wearing it. She had a suspicion that the leather the thong was cut from hadn't been cured properly, or maybe it was something even more disgusting, like catgut. The thong had been tied in a complicated knot, impossible to undo, even if anyone had been willing to touch the gross thing-thong. As for the amulet, Ella had mixed thoughts about the pendant, but it was coming with her to Scotland anyway. Ella had the vague idea of visiting the National Museum in Edinburgh to see if what Granny Campbell had told her was true: that the amulet's mate was sitting in a glass case there.

After turning the charmstone amulet over in her hand a few times, Ella decided to loop the thong around her wrist instead of wearing it over her blouse like Granny used to do.

Yes. This would be her last night in Campbell Cottage, Glenorchy. Tomorrow would see Pania driving her to Queenstown where she would catch a flight to Wellington, and then on to Sydney, Australia and Singapore, and finally, London. But for Ella, all roads and flights led to Scotland. She had a hankering to see the land of her ancestors.

***

"What's that gruesome thing around your wrist?"

Ella thought she had been lucky for the most part during her trip. The seat next to hers in New Zealand had been empty and her seat to Sydney had been so narrow that the passenger who had been mysteriously placed next to her, even though there were many empty rows and seats available on the plane, had agreed to move to another aisle the second the seatbelt sign was off. Her luck ran out flying from Singapore to London.

"It's just a family charmstone," Ella replied politely, removing her headphones from one ear.

"I thought it was a bug. Maybe a dung beetle." Her next-door neighbor for the next eight hours would be the woman sitting next to her. Like Ella, she seemed to be doing the flight on her own; unlike Ella, she seemed to want to chat. "It gave me a real shock. I don't like insects - I'm from Australia, for God's sake - all the insects in Australia want to kill you."

"It's not a scarab," Ella said politely. "It's crystal."

"What's a scarab?"

Summoning up all of her reserves of patience, Ella replied. "A dung beetle. They were held to be sacred in Egypt. Even more sacred than a cross is to a Christian."

"But you just said it's a crystal, not a scarab," the passenger reminded her. "So why is it black and smooth if it's a crystal?"

Ella held her wrist up to the reading spotlight in the ceiling. "It's more of an opaque silverish-gray actually, wouldn't you say so? I'm not sure why it was rounded into a cabochon-" Ella noticed her traveling companion open her mouth to ask another question and pre-empted it. "-a stone that's been polished and shaped round instead of cut into facets. The word comes from French for bald head. But my gran told me the stone was very old."

"Well, maybe you should take it to a jeweler for them to polish?"

Ella shook her head. "The stone was damaged once - see at the top there? - I wouldn't want to risk it being damaged again."

"Why?" This time the woman looked genuinely interested.

"Because my gran told me its twin is the Charmstone of Glenorchy."

Chapter 3

12 years before

"Hush, child," Granny Campbell crooned and clucked, patting Ella's back with a slow, steady rhythm. "My son - your dad - is in a better place. It's wrenching to know we have to wait until we see them again, but it would upset your dad if he knew you were so distraught."

Granny Campbell had found Ella in the bathroom, sitting in the corner under the cold, white, porcelain basin, with her fingers stuffed into her mouth to stop the sound of her sobs being heard. But Granny was on high alert for such behavior and soon found Ella's hiding place. Knocking softly and coming in, Granny Campbell wasted no time in sitting down on the icy tiled floor next to Ella and comforting her in the best way she could.

"Granny," Ella had wailed, "I don't think Dad can hear anything - I think he's gone. So has Mom. There might not be heaven - I don't think I *will* see them again."

Settling her knees to be more comfortable, Gran Campbell sighed. "There's more to this earth than meets the eye, Ella. When you grow up, I hope you'll understand this. No science, no physics, and no mathematical equations can explain those things that exist outside the universal sphere in which we live. Don't you think there's the possibility that your mom and dad are there - outside the sphere?"

Ella forgot her tears and knuckled her eyes as she took in what Granny was telling her. "Is heaven there?"

"I don't know," Granny said in a cheerful tone. "That's the beauty of it. It's our next great adventure. But even Albert Einstein - he was a genius professor - agreed that time and space are relative concepts. He put forward the idea that those things can be bent and folded like paper."

Taking Ella by the hand, Granny led her to the kitchen table, and after finding a notepad in one of the drawers, sat down next to Ella with a piece of blank paper in her hands. "See here, this sheet is so much more than a white rectangle shape. A few folds like this…and there you go! It's a crane bird now!"

Ella took the origami bird and inspected it from all angles. Granny showed her how she could make the wings flap, but it was not enough to distract Ella from her previous questions.

"Did that man know how to bend time and space like paper?"

"Albert Einstein? I'll tell you a fact, Ella. Some of what Mr. Einstein said is being proven correct. But we haven't gotten around to proving a few of his theories yet. I guess we were slowly catching up to him. You see, poor old science needs proof, whereas all Albert needed was his mind.

"Ella, we are here on Earth, for better or worse - bound by its rules. Tied down by its time and place in space. Imagine if we could escape those shackles. Think about finding a place where there is no time to drag us down, to make us grow weary."

"Is that heaven?" Ella wished all grownups spoke to her as her Granny Campbell did.

"Maybe. As I said, it's an adventure that comes next. Our bodies are made of chemicals - that is what you can see and touch - and electricity - that's the stuff we can't see - at its most basic level. When we die, the chemicals go back into the universe, but where does the electricity go?"

Ella pondered this for a moment and then gave her skin a pinch before saying, "But I *like* the chemicals. It's part of me. Can't I take it all with me?"

Granny had chuckled and promised to read her another chapter of The Legend of Brigadoon at bedtime. "That's my favorite," Ella had given her granny a hug. "Because falling in love made those men forget about the importance of keeping an eye on the passage of time."

"Time isn't important." Granny Campbell had huffed. "And I'll prove it. See this pendant I always wear over my blouse. The only time I ever take it off is when I bathe. It's been in my branch of the family for centuries! Thousands of months, hundreds of years, billions of seconds! Just think of that. It's meant to stay in Campbell hands or else the stone loses its power, and calamity could strike! Stories say the stone was once one whole spherical crystal that fell from the skies, but something caused the orb to split in twain and this is one half of it."

Where's the other half?" Ella wanted to know.

"In a museum in Edinburgh, but no charmstone is going to be happy if it has been sundered from its mate. Just remember that, Ella. If I pass away and this charmstone comes to you, it means you can never marry."

"What!? Why can't I marry someone, Granny?"

Isobel conceded. "Och, you can marry if you please, but you must keep your Campbell surname. Terrible bad luck will rain down on you if you forfeit your clan name - because this stone and that name are joined for all eternity."

***

Here and Now

Ella's traveling companion had listened enraptured to every word Ella had said. Even after the meal carts had come and gone, the woman wanted Ella to continue with her story in between bites.

"I wish my science teacher had made classes as interesting as that!" she told Ella when the story finished. "Have you thought about becoming a teacher?"

"Honestly," Ella took a sip of tea out of the miniature plastic cup, "I've thought about becoming an audiobook reader. So many people like to listen to books instead of reading them: their eyes are sore at the end of the day; their eyesight has been ruined from staring at a computer screen for hours on end; they find a voice lulls them to sleep."

"It can't be any worse than watching these tiny movies on this screen - five hundred films! How can they all be crappy?" the woman complained, and then went off on a rant about how bad the movies and series available on the in-flight entertainment center were. She seemed to find streaming services bad too, only to suddenly backtrack into raptures about Housewives Lives or something like that.

The only life Ella cared about was her own, but she didn't say that out loud. She didn't even have a house to live in, let alone have to be a wife inside it!

Excusing herself, Ella went to use the restroom facilities before the mad post-dinner tea, coffee, and wine dash to use the toilet formed a queue in the aisle. Ella had flown to the Gold Coast and Fiji Islands for a vacation with her friends before, so she knew the score when it came to airplane etiquette, which was basically, 'first come, first served.'

Returning to her seat, Ella was relieved to see the woman next to her had found something sufficiently banal to watch on the seat-back screen in front of her. Taking the opportunity this gave her, Ella crammed her headphones around her head and pretended to be asleep for good measure by putting her eye pads on. After a while, she didn't have to pretend at all.

***

Opting to travel from London to Edinburgh by train seemed like a good idea at the time, but Ella soon grew tired of the gnawing impatience growing inside her. It was the strangest feeling ever: if she had been younger, she might have described it as having ants in her pants. The urgent pulse surging inside her was deeply unsettling and she found it hard to concentrate.

"Anything from the tea trolley? Want a beverage?"

Ella almost snapped at the lady who pushed a cart with a hot water canteen, tea and coffee sachets, and those tiny, tin foil-capped, fake creamer pots that tourism and travel hosts around the world had decided were the ideal replacement for a jug of milk. "Er...no, thank you." Ella bit her bottom lip to stop the curse words that wanted to bubble out of her. "No, you idiot! That's the second time you've asked me! Why do you always come at the exact moment I've had to go to the food truck and fetch my own beverage five minutes ago?!"

The trolley lady stared at her and for one horrifying moment, Ella thought she might have said the words out loud. But no.

"Are those contacts? Excuse me for asking, but my daughter wants some and I was wondering if they were comfortable. Or are they high maintenance?"

Hating herself for her previous bad-tempered thoughts, Ella replied in the friendliest way. "No, but some of my friends in school had them but eventually preferred to go for laser eye surgery instead. It's like you said: high maintenance."

They chatted for a while about the tinted contact lens craze before the trolley lady said ta-da, pushing her beverage wagon on to the next occupied booth.

Ella missed her immediately. The lady had reminded her of Gran Campbell. Talking to someone else had taken her mind off the never-ending need to get to Edinburgh, get to the museum, and find out if the charmstone kept there was her own charmstone's mate.

The frantic feeling didn't stop. Ella turned up the volume on her headphones and watched the countryside flash by. It was not that different to the South Island in New Zealand. Stick a few mountains on the horizon and the green fields, gray sea, and hedgerows flashing past could be Glenorchy. Like most nineteen year olds, Ella had laughed off any suggestion she book a bus tour or plan an itinerary, like some of the tourists that landed in Glenorchy every summer had done.

A tour bus would pull up, a tour bus driver would heave themselves down the steps to stretch and yawn, and the tour operator would use the bus announcement system to instruct the passengers that they had four hours to enjoy everything Glenorchy had to offer before the bus moved on to Paradise, another little lakeside village down the road.

"But what about your safety?" Pania had asked Ella, a worried frown on her face. "How will anyone know where you are and where you're supposed to be if you don't have an itinerary?"

All Ella had done was dangle her phone in front of her cousin's face, and then wink. "Ever heard of GPS tracking?"

Ella already had her backpack strapped behind her back and was standing by the doors when the train pulled into Waverley Station, coming to a hissing stop at around four in the afternoon.

Stopping the first person she met, Ella asked him: "Do you know where Edinburgh Museum is, please? Is it still open?"

"Och, aye, 'twill be open, but ye must hustle yerself to get there. Heid oot yonder." The man pointed to a staircase that rose up to become a walkway. Taking this to mean she must move to the other side of the train station platform, Ella thanked the man and ran in the direction he had pointed. On the other side of the turnstile was a taxi rank. She ran over to the first one and asked the same question.

"Edinburgh Museum? Aye, it's still open, but ye won't get a good look 'round before they close the doors." The black taxis were the same as the ones in London, and Ella was able to use English pounds to pay the driver her fare. She wondered why the two countries chose to agree on so many things except politics.

Throwing her pack into the backseat, Ella said, "that's okay. I can always go back to the museum tomorrow. I just want to check something first."

Shaking his head the taxi driver told Ella to fasten her seatbelt. "It's only a five-minute drive awa', but I'm goin' to have to charge ye full fare."

"Fine, fine," Ella wasn't paying attention. Her face was glued to the window, watching for the museum to hove into view which in due course, it did.

"Hie, lass! Ye forgot yer change!" Ella threw a ten-pound note at the taxi driver and darted into the building, desperate to buy a ticket before the museum closed for the day.

"Entrance is free," the man at the ticket booth told her, "but you're very welcome to make a donation. However, we are-"

"Closing soon, I know." Ella was almost jumping from one foot to the other one with agitation. "I only want to see one thing, so it's okay."

The man shrugged as if to say 'it's your funeral,' but he cheered up somewhat after Ella gave a twenty-pound donation. Waving away the offer of a brochure and what her twenty-pound donation included, Ella, followed the man's directions about how to get to the Campbell charmstone display cabinet by the fastest route.

"You'll be missing out on the theatrical masks exhibition and Arctic Circle overcoats made from seal intestines," he warned her, but the ticket booth man was already talking to thin air. This is what he would tell everyone later: 'It was like I was talking to thin air.'

Passing the display dedicated to Scottish faeries - she had grown up with Granny Campbell's stories about such beings and probably knew more about the land of Tír na nÓg than the museum guide did - Ella arrived at the Glenorchy Charmstone display cabinet.

A buzzing sound was followed by an echoing static crackle: "*Attention, museum visitors. Please note that the museum will be closing in five minutes. Please make your way to the front exit; the side exits are locked. Thank you.*"

Ella ignored the intercom announcement. It wasn't as if the museum had been teeming with visitors at this time of the evening anyway. All the tourists would have made fast tracks to the pubs and every scholar would have returned home, bar a few display cabinets and museum installation die-hards who wanted to get the most out of the tour guide recordings on their headphones before chucking it in for the day.

It felt like she was alone. The only thing that existed in Ella's rapidly shrinking world was the display cabinet in front of her. She took one step closer and held her breath. Reaching out for the glass encasing the charmstone, Ella pressed her hand against the thick pane.

"Oy! No touching the display cabinets!" A security guard was clearing the halls one by one. "Move along toward the exit, please. The museum is closing."

If it had been anyone else but Ella, the security guard would have escorted her out of the building personally. There were a lot of weirdos around who would have loved to take a hammer to an ancient artifact or throw paint on a priceless painting. But as he would tell the police later, he didn't think anything was strange about the young blonde girl standing by the Campbell charmstone, and he was certain there was no one in the museum who looked as if they were following her around.

"She weren't doing no harm," he told the baffled police. "She was just touching the pane with her left hand. There's her handprint on the glass, clear as anything. I'm telling the truth. She must have slipped out the entrance when I wasn't looking."

Only Ella had not left. The moment the guard's back was turned to monitor other areas of the museum, she pressed her hand on the glass again, allowing the amulet on the thong around her wrist to dangle in front of her so that she could compare the two charms.

The Campbell charmstone was an ordinary-looking artifact, nothing splendid. Pretty much the only thing differentiating the two amulets was that Ella's had a leather thong threaded through the suspension loop, otherwise they appeared to be very similar. Upon closer inspection, Ella saw they were not exactly the same.

Her stone's casing was more battered and black and looked to be more rudimentary in craftsmanship. The strange jagged teeth that held the stone in the cabinet were the same as the frame around her own crystal, only not so evenly placed around the stone. The back plate on which the cabinet charmstone was embedded had been embellished with orange-colored coral or dark amber at the compass points, sitting at north, south, east, and west, with a few drops of silver adornment placed in between them. Ella's stone's back plate seemed to be warped as if some violent force had tried to smash it and failed.

But the biggest difference between the two amulets was the charmstone in the cabinet had the top part damaged, the part closest to the north orange embellishment, and when Ella looked closely at the charmstone around her wrist, she saw the damage matched. The crystal bulged out at the top north point slightly, as if the missing part of the cabinet stone was hiding behind it.

"Well, I'll be damned…they are perfectly matched to one another. Gran Campbell was right."

Ella became aware of her surroundings again now that her curiosity had been satisfied. Since Gran Campbell had passed away so suddenly, it had seemed like her charmstone had demanded that she come here, insisting that she stand in front of its mate long enough for them to greet one another again.

It was too late. The museum was already closed. All the lights must have been switched off because the only available illumination was coming from the charmstone display cabinet. Ella looked around to see if the staff were playing a trick on her, but could not see a thing. It didn't make sense. It was high summer - the sun shouldn't be set for another five hours. Fumbling for the phone in her pocket, Ella wanted to take a picture of the pitch-black room she had been left in, but her fingers had gone numb with cold, and fumbled as they dropped the phone out of sight onto the murky floor. It made no sound as it disappeared.

Ella felt the need to move closer to the display cabinet because now it was her refuge in the darkness. If she stepped out of the light and into the thick blackness, it would engulf her. The museum was disappearing, it was no longer something of substance. Ella screamed as the darkness pressed in all around her and she grabbed the display cabinet glass as if it was a ship's mast that could guide her to the shore.

The cabinet was gone. This time, Ella didn't bother screaming; when she looked back and saw the amulet charmstone throbbing in the dark behind her, she was compelled to obey its command. Reaching out with her left hand, Ella joined the two stones together in a magical embrace.

Chapter 4
There and Now

The water was freezing. Ella held her breath and waited for her head to bob to the surface. There was only one thing holding her down, the backpack. No one had ever asked her the question before, but it was posed to her now: do you value your life above your possessions?

It was a no-brainer. Shrugging out of the backpack straps, Ella kicked herself free of its weight. Light as air, she rose out of the icy waves. The darkness cleared immediately and she was able to hear again. The noise was an unsettling one; low pitched yells and heavy thuds, the screaming clang of metal against metal, easy to hear above the hiss and swell of the waves crashing on the beach because of its ominous cadence.

From the light in the sky, Ella guessed it was early morning. This was confirmed when she looked left and saw a red sun rising over the ocean. Ahead of her was the shoreline. On her right was where the noise was coming from, hidden from view by an outcrop of black rocks.

Paddling forward, Ella's feet touched the shallows after a few strokes. It was winter, she could feel the bite in the air and she was dressed for it because it had been a brisk mid-winter day in Edinburgh too. It was vital she climb out of the water and onto land: she was far colder under the water than above it. Only after reaching the shore would she be able to think about how to dry out her clothes.

Spluttering and shaking, Ella waded onto the beach…she wanted to climb the rocks to see what was causing those frightful sounds more than anything else, but her clothes must come first.

Untying the hooded fleece jacket she had knotted around her waist, Ella put it on. The synthetic materials had repelled a lot of moisture. Ella felt warmer immediately and when she looked at the pale sun rising higher in the sky, she got the feeling it wouldn't have the power to dry her clothes. This proved prophetic. After sending a few minutes of gray light over the horizon, the sun settled behind a thick bank of clouds and looked likely to stay there.

The alpaca wool socks under her Caterpillars were keeping her feet warm and the woven hemp Maharishi ski pants she had worn because they were too bulky to fit into her backpack had also shrugged off the saltwater.

If she calmed down long enough to think straight, Ella supposed there was no reason for her to be soaking wet because it wasn't as if she had been in the water! Wasn't she meant to be in a foutering museum?

Lucky, lucky, lucky star. She muttered the words under her breath as she blew on her hands, squeezed her long hair dry, and jumped in one spot to get her blood pumping faster. "You were born under a lucky, lucky, lucky star."

It was a mantra Gran Campbell had taught her. Any calamity or hurt that had happened to Ella for the last twelve years had been dismissed with this prompt to her memory.

She could hold back no longer. It was time to climb the rocks to see what was happening on the other side of the beach. Under the dawn's pale light, Ella saw an incomprehensibly strange sight.

Six longboats were pulled high onto the sand. The tide had obviously sucked out from underneath them, because they were settled onto the flat wet beach, surrounded by tidemarks. Higher up, a crowd of men seemed to be trying to annihilate each other, and when she looked over to the horizon on the right, a one-masted sloop ship was anchored in the bay. The seafoam was pink where it pooled around motionless bodies lying on the beach. Ella bit her knuckle when she realized what it was.

There was no way the longboats could be used for escape. It would take at least six strong men to carry one back down to the sea. What had prompted those barbaric-looking men to attack one another on this barren coast? It must have something to do with the ramshackle encampment she could see above the shoreline.

As the sun rose behind the gray clouds, Ella noticed the two clashing throngs were dressed differently: the men with their backs to the boats were dressed in kilts - proper great kilt plaids, not the polite skirts offered for sale on clan websites. Their stocky legs were encased with warm leggings and what looked like laced-up boots of soft leather tied below the knee; covering their short coats were thick leather cuirasses and over that was a heavy pelt of fur; close-fitting caps of embossed leather were set over hair cut to reach the shoulders.

The men facing the plaid kilted warriors were wearing absurd-looking outfits in a mish-mash of colors: hose and tunics in a variety of cloths and fashions, which made them look like fierce bearded men in dresses - they had cast off their furs to be more agile during the battle, because some of the men looked pale with cold. They looked like a motley crew and very disorganized compared to the doughty warriors in plaid. They must be defending their camp from the plaid wearing attackers.

It was with dawning horror Ella figured out that there would be no surrender. This was a clash to the death and it was inconceivably brutal. Some of the men in hose and tunics held some kind of short sword or long knife in each hand, flailing them around in a dervish of death for anyone who dared come within the radius. One defender at the back had a crossbow which he seemed to be wielding with deadly accuracy.

The kilted men had shields and broadswords; many of the shields had short black crossbow bolts sticking out of them. As Ella watched, one of the tallest warriors broke away from the tight affray after slaying the man in front of him with a sword stroke into the groin. Ducking a bolt that sailed a few inches over the top of his head, he flicked a sharp blade at the man with the crossbow. The knife pierced the man's throat as if it was butter on a hot summer's day.

Instinctively, Ella grasped her throat to check if it was as soft and vulnerable as that knife thrust made it feel. The skirmish was over not long after the archer was slain. Ella could not tear her eyes away as the men wearing plaid began to calmly step over and around the bodies, occasionally bending down to stick a sharp knife into a chest or neck. Sometimes a hand would flutter into the air for supplication before the knife came down, followed by a sharp-pitched guttural whine and then silence.

"Aargh!" Someone had grabbed Ella from behind. A strong hand held her arm as a bulky elbow tightened around her neck with suffocating strength. Her hand was freed and Ella struggled to escape the vice-like chokehold, but all this caused the man to do was narrow the crook of his arm. When stars of light burst into Ella's sight, she stopped struggling. She did not bother screaming, because no one would care.

The man said something to her. "I don't understand." Ella rasped out the words in a whisper, it was all she could manage with that arm pressed against her throat. The man kicked her legs with his boots, urging her to stand and walk. Holding onto the man's arm for balance with both hands, Ella wobbled toward the red-stained beach in front of the longboats; she could hardly do otherwise.

She winced as the man behind her shouted to his captain, his hot breath blasting the hair on top of her head. The tall man who had killed the crossbow archer stepped forward. Ella knew he was the captain because she recognized the word: *caiptein*.

"*Dè th' agad an sin?*" The captain sauntered closer at a leisurely pace while cleaning his sword blade with a soiled fragment of cloth.

"*Fear de na luchd-leantainn campa aca. Chan eil i gam thuigsinn.*"

The captain made an abrupt circling motion with his hand and Ella felt the arm around her neck loosen and then fall away. Ella was slightly above average height, but it seemed as if she had fallen into a world populated by giants as she stood between the two warriors. Both men must have been well over six feet by several inches.

"*Am bheil thu labhairt ar teangaidh?*" The tall captain was so close that Ella could have touched him as he inclined his head to speak to her in his deep voice. Indeed, it was too tempting not to touch him. For all she knew, she might have hit her head or fallen into the Matrix or maybe there was some other reason for this delusion. Reaching out her hand, Ella placed her fingers on his arm; the nearest part of his body that was not covered in thick leather.

Both Ella and the captain shouted. The captain jumped back, flinching away from her, his eyes wide with surprise. "Ow!" Ella shook her fingers as if she had been scalded, "You shocked-"

In a flash, the man behind Ella had wrapped his arm around her neck again and began choking her out, but the captain stepped in to pull Ella free of the strangler's arms, laughing and speaking to his friend in a joking manner. She thought she heard the name of Thor and wondered if they were Vikings.

She had proven to herself beyond doubt that the captain, and everything around her, was real. There was no question in Ella's mind that her charmstone had caused this to happen. She was probably still in Scotland, of that Ella was sure, but she was no longer in the twenty-first century. The air was too crisp and pure, and the only trace of electricity seemed to be inside her.

A peculiar sense of inevitably came over her as she waited to see what would happen.

Rubbing his arm where she had touched him with a rueful grin on his face, the captain pronounced his words slowly and carefully. "*A bheil thu gam thuigsinn?*"

Ella shook her head and risked a small smile. The two men spoke above her head for a moment before the captain tried again. "*Cogitesne me?*" What he said sounded like a cross between Italian and Latin, definitely a step in the right direction, but Ella had to shake her head again. The man standing behind her gave her a rough push, growling some words that sounded unfriendly.

"Fouter you!" Ella spun around and swore at the man, but this only caused the tall man in front of her to say, "*Me comprenez-vous?*"

Finally, the tall captain had said something she understood. "*Oui, je vous comprends, monsieur.*" Gran Campbell had insisted Ella learn French as an extracurricular lesson from grade eight onward. Gran Campbell spent hours telling her granddaughter about the Auld Alliance between the French and the Scots that had been so strong it was deemed unnecessary for the two countries to ever formally rescind it.

Learning French well enough to be fluent in it had been a costly undertaking in New Zealand, but there had been no short supply of French teachers in the South Island who were willing to tutor school kids for extra money during their two-year touring visas. In the evenings, Gran Campbell would sometimes speak French with Ella to make sure she was keeping up with her lessons. Whenever Ella asked why her Granny didn't teach her, Gran Campbell would laugh. "Because I'm a gran, not a teacher. I'll leave the homework assignments and frustration for someone else to do, thank you very much!"

The man standing behind Ella finally let her go and went to stand next to his captain. The two men gave one another puzzled glances but shrugged and seemed satisfied just to have communication. The captain folded his arms over his chest as if he wanted to protect himself from more electric shocks. "Are you with the encampment? Or are you their captive?" His French was rudimentary but understandable.

"I-I am their captive. I was their captive." Ella replied in French, knowing she would be able to explain away her odd clothes if she could claim to be a kidnap victim from a foreign land.

"Do you have any possessions on the ship?"

Ella was rapidly beginning to understand the situation, absurd as her predicament was. The sloop belonged to the men from the encampment. They had set up a base here. The Scotsmen must have attacked the camp just before dawn, taking the men by surprise.

"I have nothing," Ella replied sadly, thinking about her backpack at the bottom of the sea. "Are we in the Land of the Scots?"

"Did they not tell you?" the captain frowned as Ella shook her head. "You are standing on the Isle of Bonawe in Loch Etive. From whence did they take you?"

"Loch? Is this not a sea?" Lifting her fleece to her nose, Ella sniffed. It was definitely seawater or at least very briny water.

"At the top of the loch," the man pointed left, "it is water. At the bottom," he gestured toward the waters where the sloop was anchored, "it is salt."

Ella's pattering heartbeats stilled as she heard the cry of gulls circling around her. She didn't like to think what smell had caught the birds' interest; the waves lapping the beach sand were still salmon pink with blood.

The two men began to talk amongst themselves again. It was bizarre to Ella that they could be acting so casually after annihilating over thirty human beings. Where was the grief counseling? Where was the PTSD? The psych evaluation? These thoughts made Ella snort with laughter, even as she stood on the beach shivering in front of the same men who treated death so casually. The captain looked at her as she stood there, shaking and laughing in what Ella had to admit was a hysterical way.

"Do you wish to return to your own land?" All Ella could do after the captain asked her that question was laugh even louder while shaking her head. "No, no, no." She kept repeating the word over and over. The captain shrugged before taking Ella's arm and walking her toward one of the longboats, where he removed his gray wolf pelt cape and wrapped it around her shoulders. It was so long, it almost reached her ankles.

There was a small jolt when he touched her and Ella knew he felt it too, but the electricity had lost some of its power. "Do you worship Thor? You are Norse, yes?" Saying this, the man reached up and touched her hair, running the silken strands through the fingers of his large hand.

She wanted to tell him that she was Scottish once long ago. Her ancestors must have wandered these rolling hills and stared up at those sullen, snow-capped mountains, but all Ella could do was mutter. "No, no, no." Her confusion was palpable.

Walking her down to the longboat, the captain splashed into the icy water as if it were a hot spring. Ella hesitated at the edge of the shore, the memory of the water's chill bite still fresh in her mind. Accepting her reluctance with patience, the captain turned around and waded back to where she was standing. He said nothing, just held out his arms for her. Ella wrapped her arms around his neck as he hefted her legs up. Everything about this man was rough and outlandish, but yet somehow so familiar to her. As he carried her to the longboat, wading easily through the knee-high water that lapped over his soft leather boots, Ella knew what it must be like to weigh nothing at all.

She supposed her body weight would not mean much to someone used to lugging a shield and broadsword around with them everywhere and this was no time to indulge in how delightful it felt to be held tightly to a man's chest, most especially a man who looked like this one.

After placing her onto one of the wooden slats across the longboat's hull, the captain trudged back to shore to select the men he wanted to row. Only then did Ella regain some of her composure. A fatalistic calm flooded over her as she realized it was highly likely that she was here for the long haul. This was no flash in the pan; these hills and lakes were her new reality.

Ella supposed the vessel wasn't a true Viking-type longboat however the shape was similar to one. A mast lay in the middle of the boat with a thick canvas sail wrapped around it and there was no prow on the bow, but it had the same feel as a longboat, especially after five men followed the captain into the water and climbed into the boat after him.

One of the men crept over to the bench where Ella was sitting and grunted, pointing at the boat bottom where the rowers were placing their feet. Carefully moving to sit on the floorboards, Ella crouched cross-legged beside the man's knees, using the time the men took to launch the boat to remove the damp ski pants from her legs. She had on a pair of lycra cotton blend leggings underneath that would protect her from the cold while her pants dried off.

As she tied her bootlaces again, Ella saw a few of the men point at her, snickering amongst themselves. Seeing this, the captain came to take the seat opposite the rower and beckoned Ella to sit on top of the sail-wrapped mast in the middle of the boat, which she did with one leg on either side.

"You sit like a man." Lifting up the oar, the captain waited for the man in the bow to give the signal for the rowers to begin.

"It's how women sit where I come from," Ella was well satisfied with her story so far. She knew about the kind of places that were obscure enough for her to be able to pass off her Caterpillar hiking boots, pale blue mid-thigh length oversize tee-shirt, and fleece jacket as regional curiosities. What was that exhibition she had walked past at the museum? Seal intestines. The garment in that display looked a bit like waterproof polyester.

Pulling on the oar as the bowman shouted out orders, the captain seemed to think about her reply for a long while, but Ella was soon to find out that this was only until the longboat was clear of the island shoreline. When she turned to see in front of them, Ella noticed the boat was heading fairly rapidly toward a river mouth. She pointed at the river mouth. "Bonawe?" He seemed ready to converse with her again. The man shook his head. "River Awe."

Ella had to agree. The scenery was awesome. The weak sunlight trapped behind the clouds turned the brush under the bare tree branches russet red. Not all the trees were affected by the season; as she looked up at the snowy mountains in the distance, Ella could see pine tree green. It was as if the men in the boat reflected the landscape with their russet hair and gray woolen plaids. She risked giving an appraising look at the man beside her.

"What name do they call you, Captain?" If he thought she sat like a man, she might as well be forward like one too, and ask him leading questions.

Pulling on the oar, his arm muscles bulging out of the snug woolen sleeve laced tightly to the coat under his cuirass, the man shook his head. "You are the stranger, you must give your name first."

So, she must be on his land. That is why they had attacked and slaughtered the men from the sloop; they had been encroaching. "I call myself Ella Campbell."

The man almost dropped his oar. Calling to the bowman, he came to sit opposite Ella on the mast after the bowman had taken his place at the oar. "You are no clan of mine. Why do you lie?"

The curiosity had disappeared from his eyes; the man had a ferocious scowl on his face now. Ella's heart was in her throat. One misstep and she would most probably be tossed overboard without so much as one tear of regret. "I am a slave! Born into slavery. Campbell was my mother's name."

Ella was praying that a Campbell woman had disappeared twenty-odd years ago whom they might be able to hypothesize was her mother. She bit her lip, waiting for his reaction. Instead, he lifted her hand and began to inspect the rounded fingernails and pink fingertips. "You do not have a slave's hands." He waited, watching Ella's face intently to see if he could detect a lie.

Thanking her lucky stars once again that she never had time to get false nails and polish - Glenorchy was not exactly a Mecca for manicurists - Ella was emboldened to reply. "Those men, they had me for a short time. I was to cook their food."

It was the only job Ella could imagine no seafaring man would want to do once they reached land and set up camp. Releasing her hand, the captain asked. "Did they not use you for pleasure?"

In a stroke of genius, Ella shook her head. "Thor protects me," holding out her hand toward him, she mimicked an electric shock. "Lightning, yes?"

Yes. He understood, and even better, he looked to be amused. "I need such prayers, lady. I need such tricks." They laughed together for a short while, each one finding comfort in the lightness that comes after death and destruction. "I am Callum," he placed his hand on his chest in a courtly gesture. "Callum Campbell. Once we reach Kilchurn, I will send for your people."

Ella didn't try to dissuade him. She wanted to get to dry land before she attempted to think of her next lie.

Trying to get comfortable with her back against the hard wooden slat and with the mast tucked between her legs, Ella watched the river slide past. It was a very peaceful way to travel; there was no rocking or noise except the swish of oars in the water. She thought the men must be incredibly strong until she realized the tidal waters from the inlet where she had landed must be pulling them inland. Steep hillsides marched on the left side of the water; as they approached, Ella saw a hawk or an eagle glide up from the river's surface, clutching a fish between its claws.

The boats continued to hug the left side of the river as the bow-man guided the rowers to hold to the portside, following what Ella thought was the main tributary. Only it wasn't. As the pale noontime sun shone weakly down on her from directly above, the water opened out all around her, spreading into a wide, black surface that winked and lapped like an endless pot of ink on every side of the boat.

As a vast stone tower hoved into view, standing alone on a rocky peninsula toward the northeastern side of the loch, Ella heard the captain say, "*Chez moi.*" Home.

Chapter 5

"Send word to Sir Colin - we are returned." The captain ordered one of the urchins who was watching Ella with gape-mouthed fascination as she clambered out of the boat, gingerly placing her boot into the shallow loch waters with a shudder. Ella only heard the 'Sir Colin,' part and was pleased to think she had managed to decipher those two words amidst all the others. It was a start. Her great-uncle had also been Colin Campbell, and he had pronounced his name in exactly the same way. At least there was some consistency in that.

"*Est-il votre père?*" she asked the captain, desperately hoping the semi-demolished castle and the half-a-dozen wooden cottages dotted around it would have a fireplace where she could dry her boots and alpaca wool socks.

He shook his head in her direction after giving his men orders to carry the boat further up the shore. "Nay. Sir Colin is not my father. He is my uncle. I am his foster son."

Ella tried not to look astonished by the man's sudden burst of eloquence, or at least it was as talkative as such a dour bunch of warriors could hope to be. As she grew more aware of her surroundings, Ella noticed parts of the castle looked to be under construction. Another small boy who had been making use of his time fishing in the loch came forward holding a black horse and reeking of fish guts. Ruffling the boy's hair, Callum took the horse's halter and swung himself up onto the saddle after allowing the boy to help him untie and remove his cuirass. He positioned himself as far back against the high saddle cantle as possible before reaching out his hand for Ella to use to mount and sit in front of him. "Fear not," he said, correctly gauging the reluctance in her eyes. "There is space enough."

One of the soldiers made a loud remark in Callum's direction which sent the men chuckling. The captain chuckled too, but shook his head with a wry smile on his face.

"What is so humorous?" Ella wanted to know, still eyeing the saddle with misgiving. She had experience with the ponies on her uncle's farm in Glenorchy, but this horse was exceptionally tall and seemed to like tossing its head and shaking its mane in a disconcerting way.

"They are uncouth men, lady," Callum said, still holding his hand out for her to catch hold of, "pay them no mind." Ella's temper peeked through, despite her desperate circumstances. "I think I should be the judge of how uncouth it is! After all, I seem to be the subject of the joke!"

 Callum regarded her steadily before seeming to relent. "He said that you are lucky the Campbell men have forsworn the wearing of a codpiece under our garb - else you might not fit in front of the saddle with me."

The captain called it a braguette in French, but Ella had read enough medieval manuscripts to know what he meant when he said it: the protective pouch tucked between the hose that was meant to cover - and sometimes even emphasize - the male member. She blushed a furious red and shot daggers at him, overwhelmed with shyness until she saw the kindness in Callum's eyes. "I told you it was uncouth, lady. Must I beg you to pardon me for being its mouthpiece?"

Feeling silly, Ella replied lightly, "I dare swear there is no need to hide what nature made when it is hidden under your-" not knowing the French word for pleated plaid, she rubbed the cloth of his great kilt between her fingers instead, resting her wrist on his knee as she did so.

Ella did not know whether to be pleased or dismayed when his more relaxed manners left him and he became withdrawn. Looking around the small wooden structures clustered around the castle foundations, Ella guessed the man's interactions with women must be limited out of necessity. Or maybe he was tired of experiencing the frisson of electricity that sparkled between them.

When she looked at the saddle, she saw there was a narrow gap between the captain's plaid-draped crotch and the pommel. She took his hand and allowed him to pull her up, placing her legs on either side of the saddle after clambering on top. The pommel pushed in between her legs in the most disconcerting way, but Ella was sure she would prefer riding to see Sir Colin instead of walking there. She felt exhausted and drained, more than sitting in a boat and climbing out of a freezing loch might explain away.

She heard more laughter coming from the soldiers. "What now?" Ella sighed with exasperation. The captain was tall enough for her head to fit neatly beneath his chin; she felt his voice rumble in his chest as he answered her curtly. "You ride like a man too."

With the captain's arms on either side of her, Ella's neck jolted back as he spurred the horse into a canter. There were no half-measures for this man; he either took everything at his leisure or at a crazy pace. Her head was bouncing around so much, all she could do was watch with a sort of fascinated horror at how quickly the ground was disappearing underneath the horse's hooves.

Together, they traveled swiftly around the brow of the hill, using a sidetrack that allowed them to avoid the sprinkling of snow that had settled on the barren knoll. They reached a grand three-storied manor house situated on a sloping dell behind the hill amidst a scattering of trees. It had been built out of the same gray stone and black slate as the castle: there was a raised arch gatehouse entrance with what looked like barracks and stables on either side of it. Inside the cobbled court-yard, Ella saw the main manor house in front of her, with its steeply gabled roofs and narrow shuttered windows. The house was either below the line of snowfall or else protected by the dell. It looked magnificent and cozy at the same time. At least the manor looked cozier than a saddle and a boat was Ella's firm estimation.

An ostler ran out to lead the horse away to wooden stables adjoining the western wall after the captain had lifted her clear of the saddle.

"The dye used to color your hose must have cost your master one year's worth of gold." Ella struggled to understand the statement because he used the English word for hose: hosa. When he saw her incomprehension, he ran his hand along her thigh and then pointed to her thin denim leggings. The action was not an affectionate one: Ella could see the look of wonder on Callum's face as he inspected the blue color of her cheap, no-name brand denim leggings - the kind with an elasticized waistband instead of a zipper, and no pockets. Tired of lies, Ella chose to stay silent. She just shrugged and shook her head, a gesture that seemed to encapsulate how she felt since her head had broken through the water at dawn.

Somehow, rumor of her strange appearance had preceded El-la's arrival. The doors were open and a crowd of servants were clustered around it, jibber-jabbering excitedly amongst themselves. Callum pointed for Ella to go ahead of him. Straightening her shoulders, Ella walked under a kind of porch or mud room area with a floor of flagstone thickly covered in thresh reeds, and then into the great hall entrance by way of pushing aside heavy tapestries hanging from the arching ceiling beams.

Straight in front of her was a stone dais with several men and women sitting behind the heavy, carved table. The man seated in the middle of the dais table had a neutral expression on his face which made Ella think she might be in the presence of someone who knew how to mask his true thoughts under a veneer of diplomacy. Feeling Callum prodding her back, Ella walked forward. Thinking something more than simply standing would be required of her, Ella bowed.

She heard Callum announce her as he stood behind. "Sir Colin-" she didn't understand the rest of his announcement, but it sounded incredibly descriptive and eloquent. Ella wished with all her heart she had learned Gaelic, but then realized how lucky she was to understand the scant French with which the captain and she had been conversing in.

"Thank heaven for small mercies," she whispered under her breath.

The man seated in the middle of the long table on top of the dais held up his hand and said something. "What did you just say?" Callum asked her. "My uncle, Sir Colin, wants to know."

"I-I was praying…I spoke in my own language," Ella desperately wanted to stop telling lies. She had watched enough cop shows in her time to know that the more intricate the lies became, the easier it was to catch the liar.

"And what language is that?" Callum translated for his uncle.

Ella had a sneaking suspicion that she should distance herself from speaking Norse: there was a strong likelihood that this close to Sweden or Norway someone who understood Norse would be within traveling distance. "The Urals. I speak the language of the people to the north of the Rus." That was about as distant as she could imagine. If Sir Colin produced a traveler from the Ural Mountain range now, she would take it as a sign that she was meant to be caught out.

"Sir Colin wishes to know why is it that you don't speak our tongue if your mother was Campbell? Or the tongue of your Norse slavemaster?"

Good questions, Ella thought as she searched her brain for a good answer. "My mother died at birth. All she left me was my name. I was brought up by a Ural slave. She did my speaking for me, so I was never encouraged to speak Norse. Then I was bonded to a French merchant…but-but I strayed too far from the house and was taken captive by those men."

"Sir, and most honorable Uncle," Callum made his request politely. "May we speak French? The conversation will go all the quicker for it. This woman speaks the Gallic tongue strangely, but there is meat on its bones that a man is able to flesh out with his understanding."

Sir Colin leaned forward with his elbows on the table and addressed Ella directly. "Why are you dressed like a man?"

The woman beside him whispered in Sir Colin's ear. He held up his hand toward the woman with the palm facing out. "Aye. Lady Margaret makes a worthy point: it is told that you do all things like a man. What is the reason for this?"

Sweeping his hand to indicate Ella from head to toe, a few interested observers who had wandered into the hall during Ella's interrogation whispered to one another, and there was some tittering laughter.

The enormity of what had happened to her struck Ella with great force. She was meant to be in the Edinburgh Museum in the evening time during the early years of the second decade of the twenty-first century. And now she was here. As the walls began to spin around, all Ella could think was that fainting was something that happened to other people, not her.

"Be wary! The lady is falling." Sir Colin commented in his neutral voice as if he was talking about the time of day. There was no need for him to alert Callum. The captain caught Ella before she hit the reeds that were scattered over the flagstone floor.

***

"Hush, lady," a female voice spoke softly as Ella opened her eyes. "Do not think to rise; you are much fatigued. I believe an ague grips your body." A pewter mug was brought to her lips for Ella to sip. It tasted like beer-flavored water.

Ella could not tell if it was evening time or the early morning of the next day. All she could focus on was that she was still inside the manor house belonging to Sir Colin Campbell, which meant she was still there or here, wherever 'here' might be. A small fire burned in the grate; enough to warm the small room and make it almost cheerful.

"What time is it?" she asked the young girl who was bending over the makeshift bed on which Ella lay. The girl shook her head, not understanding. Racking her brain to think of what term she might use to pose the question in a way that it might be understood, Ella tried again. No wonder the girl probably believed her to have brain fever: not only was she having to translate everything into schoolgirl French before she said it, but Ella was struggling with the right words to use too!

"What bell has rung? Is it morning or night?"

The girl smiled. "The manor house burns candles, lady. We have not yet been blessed with a kirk bell tower. Six candles have guttered since midnight. Does this help you?"

Ella nodded and smiled back to show her gratitude. "Yes, I thank you. When was I brought-" she pointed to the four heavily tapestried walls around her, "-here."

"My brother's soldiers arrived a little after dinner yesterday. You were with them. He told us that you flung yourself into the loch when his men attacked the brigands' camp." The girl giggled, covering her mouth with her hand. "What is so droll?" Ella wanted to know, but the girl blushed and shook her head. Still, she answered once her mirth had abated. "My brother told us that you must have been using the loch as a latrine a moment before his soldiers' arrival, and…and he said you were in the right place to shit yourself with fear if that is what you were so inclined to do!"

Ella fumed quietly, biting back the acid comment she wanted to make about Captain Callum's lack of finesse. Fortunately, the night-gown she was wearing distracted her because Ella could sense she was naked underneath it.

Sitting up, she fingered the linen undergarment. The material was crisp and clean to the touch. "Where are my clothes?" Ella wanted to know. They were her last link to the museum and the display cabinet. To the average passerby in London, Ella knew they would consider her clothes to be standard student fare: hoodie fleece, enormous baggy tee-shirt so long it reached her thighs, lycra sports bra, panties, and her precious alpaca wool socks and Caterpillar boots. Now she was wearing a loose beige smock.

"Sir Colin ordered for your tunic, cote, and hose to be brought before him," the girl whispered after darting a cautious look toward the door, "But I kept your small clothes here, deeming them too… fragrant to place before our uncle." Rising from the low stool she had been sitting on, the girl retrieved Ella's underwear from where they had been hidden in a wooden chest pushed against the wall on the far side of the room.

The lycra sports bra and panties looked alien to Ella as the girl gave them to her. Was her previous life slipping away from her already? What would Sir Colin think of her denim leggings, long baggy tee-shirt, and hoodie fleece? Was her expensive hemp ski pants still in the boat?

"Your bindings and loincloth are fragile," the girl remarked, "you are lucky your breasts and arse are pert."

It was said in a practical and calm manner, but still, Ella blushed. Like every schoolchild to ever learn French, of course, she had mastered the swear words first.

I suppose the remnants of Victorian-era morals and speech are so deeply embedded into Kiwi culture that we are no longer even aware of it.

Unaware of Ella's inner thoughts, the girl amended her words. "Beg pardon, lady," the girl said, noticing Ella's fiery cheeks. "Did the brigands force you to bind your breasts for a reason? Was your master jealous to share your charms with the others?"

Giving herself a small shake, Ella moved to stand up. "Never mind that - I can assure you that all those men are dead. What name are you called by?" she asked the girl, "You say Callum is your brother." Shyly, the girl pushed a pewter chamber pot toward Ella and pointed to the wash bowl in the corner as she tucked the truckle bed back under the main poster bed on the dais. Ella squatted over the pot and was pleased to see she was not dehydrated. The water in the wash bowl was freezing enough to wake her up, and she used a frayed wool cloth to wipe the last traces of sleep - and the last remnants of her mascara - off her face.

The questions had distracted the girl away from asking about Ella's supposed enslavement. She moved to the chest to remove a tightly spun woolen tunic dress and then brought it back to where Ella was standing, to measure it against the length of her legs. "Och aye, lady, I mean, yes. Callum is my brother. He placed you in my care because I have been schooled in French. I can read too. I am not fostered to Sir Colin though - I am here for my betrothal. I am called Margaret."

Ella smiled as she remembered the Middle Ages and its propensity for naming all females the same. "I understand those words: 'och aye.' I like those words. Teach me some more of your language."

Margaret shook her head. " I dinnae think I can, lady. We speak such a disorder of Gaelic, Anglish, and Cumbric, not even our neighboring clans can understand us. My brother, Callum, learnt Latin with our cousins - so that he can read the Bible to me."

Margaret indicated that she wanted to lift the woolen tunic over Ella's head. Ella lifted up her arms and bent forward, straightening up to allow the soft, shapeless tunic to fall to past her knees.

"You are so tall, lady, I must tack a hem onto the tunic before it is ready for you. I would swear your father was Norse. Before she died, did your mother tell your foster mother who fathered you? He must have been a great Viking." Margaret seemed happy to chat in her inconsequential way.

"The men' 'round these parts are not so short," Ella made polite conversation as Margaret bent to measure how much cloth must be added to the tunic. "Callum is big enough-" Cutting herself off, Ella realized she had just been about to make a modern comparison about Captain Callum - 'big enough to play forward in a rugby scrum' had been the words on her lips. The only thing that had stopped her was that she hadn't known the French words for rugby scrum. "Big enough to lift one of the castle tower stones up," she finished saying lamely. Fortunately, Margaret seemed content to accept the praise of her brother's physical prowess.

"Aye, lady, Callum is strengthy. His mother was from the land of the Norse. A great lady. Our faither was also large, but my mother was petite. So, the height did not come to me."

Ella committed the word 'faither' to her shortlist of new words. She guessed that with so many women dying in childbirth, a man might have any number of wives in his lifetime. "How many years do you have, Margaret?" She guessed the girl must be about sixteen, despite her diminutive size and an appearance that made Ella suppose the girl might not even have her periods yet: what did they call it? Lunar cycle? The womanly time of the moon? "I have twelve years, lady," Margaret told her proudly.

"Fouter!" Ella gasped. "When are you to be betrothed!?"

Margaret seemed to think it was better to pay no attention to Ella's shocked reaction. "When my uncle finds the right man for me," she replied, accepting her life for how it was. "I must go find a length of wool for the hem, lady." And on those words, she was gone.

***

By the time Margaret had attached the sash of wool to her hem, Ella had drunk all of the small beer the girl had brought her earlier that morning. She was starving, but Margaret didn't seem to understand the French word for petit déjeuner - breakfast. Frowning to understand, Margaret said, "You want to be small and young? I wish that for you too, lady, because then I would not have to amend your tunic."

Giving up politeness, Ella stated the truth. "I have hunger."

Yes. There was a slight gnawing sensation in her gut for something other than food, and Ella had the unsettling feeling that it might be an urge to see Callum again. Biting off the end of the thread after tucking her bone needle safely back into the trunk, Margaret stood up, looking very satisfied. "I will take you to the kitchens for bread and cheese. Dinner is later."

There were no mirrors, so Ella looked down at the long tunic that stopped a few inches above her ankles. Margaret had coaxed a pair of the tight wool hose onto Ella's legs and fixed them to a soft, thin leather belt tied around her waist under the linen chemise Ella had been wearing when she woke up. A pair of leather slippers with pointed toes were pulled onto her feet. Next came a braided leather rope tied around her waist. Margaret searched in the trunk once more and came back with a silk pouch that she attached to the belt. The finishing touch was a linen hood that Margaret fixed around Ella's head with a crooked pin after rigorously scraping back Ella's hair into it.

Paying close attention to her garb, Ella asked Margaret what year of our Lord was it. "My memory is confused you see, Margaret, since those brigands took me captive."

"The year is - I misremember how to say it - my brother writes it thus."

Margaret went back to her trusted chest and returned with a parchment letter that had the seal broken. Using one corner of the precious parchment after spreading it out on the floor and kneeling beside it, Margaret used a charcoal stylo to write on it: MCDLII.

Chapter 6

The year was 1452. How could this be? Yesterday, she had been staring into a display cabinet in the Edinburgh Museum and today she was standing in the bedchamber of a fifteenth century manor house next to a loch. Ella might have believed herself to have lost her mind if everything was not so real around her.

And then there was her childhood which had literally been packed full of time travel myths and legends: stories in which the rules of space and the measure of time were suspended, almost always irrevocably. It was as if Gran Campbell had known this would happen when the charmstones met each other.

But why here? Why now?

Her long-sleeved tee shirt was gone, so Ella's wrists were exposed every time she moved her arms to poke out of the wool tunic. Ella slid the charmstone off her wrist and pulled it over her neck instead. Her hatred of the manky leather thong was gone now that she had an inkling of how old the charmstone might actually be and what its purpose was.

She asked Margaret to tighten the tunic laces over her shoulders to bring the neckline up higher.

"If you are worried for your collarbones to be showing, lady, I can drape an earasaid around your shoulders and throat. That will be both warm and modest." Thinking about what a stone castle would be like in the middle of winter, Ella accepted the long wool shawl gratefully and began to hope she could stay warm once Margaret placed Callum's wolf pelt cloak over all the other clothes she had on. "Do you not need these warm clothes for yourself, Margaret?" she asked the young girl.

"Och nay, lady," Margaret checked to see that Ella had understood the words she had just said before continuing after Ella smiled and nodded. "Callum told me that he would command the weavers to make me as many beautiful tunics and shifts as I wanted - and pay for them too - if only I dressed you in womanly garb."

Ella laughed. "I'm sure I am much obliged to him! And to you, Margaret."

When Margaret had said her brother's name, that strange tugging sensation happened to Ella again. It was a cross between a stomach flip and a surge of excitement inside her chest; it heightened her senses and made her feel more alive.

It must be because he is the first person I was able to speak to, or maybe it's because he also felt that power, that electric shock between us. I don't seem to have that effect on anyone else.

Following Margaret down the dark corridor lit by the gray dawn light coming through the narrow grated windows, Ella saw the floorboards were made of timber and knew that Margaret's bedchamber was not at ground level. She had no idea whether that was a reflection on Margaret's status as Sir Colin's niece - or whether Sir Colin had plans to use his niece as a bargaining chip during her betrothal.

"Where are we going?" Ella wanted to know. Margaret was most forthcoming. "I am taking you to Lady Margaret in the solarium. She does not think kindly of you and has great influence over our laird. When Callum saw Lady Margaret's revulsion at your arrival and foreign manners, he became most anxious that you ingratiate yourself with the Lady."

Ella put a hand on Margaret's arm. "Tell me more. I beg you."

The young girl sucked her lower lip as she recollected what her brother had told her. "Well...lady, you confess to being a slave, most likely born out of wedlock. There's that. And you were dressed as a man in a short tunic and hose in unmaidenly colors...colors you had no right to be wearing due to your lowly status. And your hair was on show for all the men to see. One of our ladies said that your jerkin looked to be made from uncured furry fish guts - and it had a miniature ladder sewn into it! If I were to see such a thing, I, too, would be scandalized. But your poulaines cause the biggest outrage; they appeared to be assembled by the gods' blacksmith."

"I thought you were Christians," Ella said in a dry tone, her mind busy concocting lies to explain away all the things that Lady Margaret did not like about her. "You told me that Callum learnt Latin so that he might read the Bible. How would anyone know that Vulcan or Brokkr make shoes?"

Margaret tossed her head in a regal manner, replying with some severity. "We refer to the old ways on occasion, lady, as did Lady Margaret when she saw your poulaines." Ella hurriedly apologized for her questioning the household's piety. Margaret curtsied and stepped aside, allowing Ella to enter the solarium first.

Keeping the girl's curtsy in mind, Ella bent her knees and held her tunic forward with one hand as she bowed her head. She did it the moment she stepped over the threshold. Maintaining a demure expression, Ella made eye contact with the lady of the manor for the second time in her life.

Lady Colin Campbell had the face of a woman who liked to reserve her expressions for when she was behind closed doors. Although the skin was beginning to thin with age on her motionless face, there were hardly any lines on it. This gave the lady an almost transparent appearance. She had heavy-lidded eyes; the same bland eyes as the numerous medieval paintings Ella had seen in books. It was a while before Ella saw the hooded lids came from the lady's sleepy demeanor: her eyes did not have hooded lids - they just looked like that because Lady Campbell had her eyes only half open in her still face. Her hair was scraped back into a rigorously tight bun under a close-fitting cap. The tightness of the lady's hairstyle gave her facial features a stretched-out look, all the more noticeable because of the pallor of her skin.

An elderly lady of high rank stepped forward to greet Ella in the same manner, then she pointed to a stool that was pushed up against the wall. Feeling humbled, Ella sat down on the stool.

"Nay, nay," the elderly lady-in-waiting explained, "Pick up the stool and bring it closer. Place it there, there! At Milady's feet."

Dithering around, Ella eventually sat down, trying to think of how a lady might do it. The stool was so low, her knees rose in front of her like wool-covered hills. Putting her feet neatly together, Ella placed her hands on her lap and waited. At least the lady-in-waiting seemed to speak a kind of rudimentary French.

"Of what station was your mither?" the elderly lady asked Ella after receiving the question from Sir Colin's wife.

Trying not to seem as if she was thinking about her words carefully before saying them, Ella replied. "My...mither died before I knew her, only leaving her clan name behind for me to inherit."

"Was Campbell your mither's clan or your faither's clan?"

Sternly suppressing a shrug, Ella pulled a sorrowful face and raised her hands to show empty. The universal sign for 'I don't know.'

The ladies chattered amongst themselves for a while, staring at Ella and not bothering to hide their inquisitiveness. Ella found their inspection very unnerving, not knowing what was waiting at the end of it. The lady-in-waiting stood up from her chair and went out of the room, so Ella felt at ease enough to look around her as the other ladies ignored her and went back to their embroidery.

The solarium was a comfortable room, clearly a space where only people of high status were permitted to congregate. A medium-sized grate held a well-stocked fire, burning brightly with crackling flames. Instead of stones, the walls on one side were covered in wrought, highly decorative woodwork; the other wall held an enormous tapestry.

The scene woven into the wall hanging was one of the Greek myths, possibly Artemis hunting with her maidens and dogs. The outside-facing wall was covered with tight skins of tanned animal hide to keep out any winter drafts that might try to sneak past the wooden shutters. One of the ladies saw her staring around the room.

"You like? Tu aime? Is the same at Norse?"

It was a mix of French and highly Scots-inflected English. Ella just nodded, too shy to answer back in the few words of Campbell clan language that she knew. She memorized the words: you like-you like-you like. Saying them over and over again to imprint the phrase in her memory. Ella wanted to say a few words of Scots to Callum when she saw him again.

Eventually, the lady returned, holding Ella's Caterpillar boots and fleece jacket in her arms. Lady Campbell signaled for the items to be placed on the side table standing against the tapestry wall.

The lady held up one boot, waiting for another sign from Lady Campbell. After the woman had nodded her head in the same sleepy fashion as she did most things, her lady-in-waiting posed the question: "What are these poulaines? Where did you get them?"

Ella had realized that the easiest way to get out of providing an honest answer would be to blame the brigands for every inexplicable thing. Dead men cannot talk.

"The brigands - the ones Captain Callum killed - they gave them to me." Before the lady-in-waiting could pick up the fleece jacket and ask her the same question, Ella preempted it. "They attired me in all the clothes I was wearing."

All the ladies broke out with their opinions about this latest bit of information. Amazingly, Ella was able to follow the gist of the conversation this time because of the word they were using: diabhal. The devil. Immediately, Ella put the most angelic look on her face, striving for a nice blend of pious and pure. Did they burn witches at the stake during the Medieval times? Or did that only start after the publication of the Maleficus Maleficarum? That notorious book about how to find and kill witches.

Her imagination started on a route Ella wished with all her heart she had never begun to think about: medieval tortures used to extract information and cruel deaths as punishment.

The wheel - breaking the person's legs and arms so they could be threaded through the spokes of a cart's wheel. The breaking had to be done by a professional so the person did not die from shock, as the aim was for the punishment to last for many days. Who would break a butterfly on that wheel of torture, never mind a human being? What crazed mind had created such things?

The gibbet - hanging the victim in a cage at the crossroads and waiting for them to starve to death. The rotting corpse and bones would be left in the cage as a grim warning.

The Pear of Anguish - a pear-shaped contraption placed into an orifice and slowly screwed wider and wider…

The Judas Cradle, Death by Rats, the Knee Splitter, the Press…

Ella was not even aware that she had let out a terrified sob. The ladies stopped chatting to stare at her.

"Why is it that you cry?" the lady-in-waiting acted at Lady Campbell's mouthpiece again.

It was a form of torture having to think about the words she needed to use and translate them into French before she could say them, but Ella tried hard to calm herself enough to do so. "I-I am innocent - *innocent!*"

The words were the same in both French and English. "*Neo-chiontach.*" the lady-in-waiting translated for the others. "Aye, girl. Our Lady Campbell agrees that those brigands must have been in league with the devil, and dressed you according to their lights. Have you hunger? You are free to go down to the kitchens - find Christian nourishment to put some roses in the face."

That she was free to go gradually sunk down into Ella's brain. Her initial impulse was to jump up and run for the door, but she managed to restrain herself. She stood up slowly and curtsied. Only after straightening up did Ella begin walking backwards to the door, feeling for the latch with her fingers behind her back. She wasn't sure if the lady had granted her permission to go seek out food or whether she had been instructed to go and read the Bible, but Ella wanted to make good her escape while she could. Maybe she should hide her ability to read too: who knew what dire punishment that might rain down on her...

"Stay!" The lady-in-waiting tilted her head to the side as she listened to Lady Campbell's whispered command. Ella quailed, but kept her serene pose, turning back with an inquiring look on her face. "Milady tells me that you must stay down in the kitchen from now on. You are an escaped slave. You must earn your bread and milk with your labor. Now you can go."

The relief coursing through her veins at the realization she would not be burnt at the stake rapidly dissipated as she wandered around the castle passages, looking for the kitchens. It was almost pitch black in every passage and Ella tried to remember what time the sun began to set in Scotland in mid-winter. She needed to find someone who could tell her where Loch Awe was on the map, if they had maps in 1452 that was. Wishing that Margaret would come back and show her around, Ella guessed that she would be too far below Callum and his sister in status now for them to bother their heads over her. Still, Ella tried to be cheerful about her new situation: it was better to be a servant than a prisoner or a victim.

Her meandering route ended abruptly as she exited out of what turned out to be a large window casement shutter. It led out onto the narrow battlement wall that encased the manor house courtyard. Poking close to her neck behind her was a roof of closely fitted pieces of slate kept in place with mortar.

Ella gasped as she saw the panoramic view all around her. From the gatehouse, barracks, and stables below her to the countryside beyond the walls, Loch Awe was astonishingly beautiful. It forced her to stop and turn to look at the rolling hills and snowcapped mountains surrounding the dell. It was all too magnificent, and had the power to still the hunger pangs in her belly, stopping Ella's search for food in its tracks.

It sank in gradually as Ella came to see how much she had missed on the boat ride up the loch. She was not concerned about this: it was not every time that someone was ripped out of their time and place in space.

Nothing could have prepared Ella for the sheer clean loveliness of the place. Her previously formed concepts about mid-fifteenth-century domiciles being cesspits of fly-covered latrines and sloppy chamber pots being thrown out of windows faded away.

The sky was gray and the clouds hung low, so heavy they were with sleet or icy rainfall. As she watched, Ella saw lighter, whiter mist wisping toward the dell, slowly pushing between the hills on its way to envelope the manor house with smoke-like fingers. The lands around the grounds had been cleared and a few hardy, long-haired goats were seen grazing the smaller slopes. It was not a green land: the grass and bushes were browned to a crisp by frostbite. Even the ferns and lichen on the jagged outcrops of silver rocks poking out of the soil seemed to have been tarnished by the winter weather. Shivering as the crisp air probed under her woolen tunic, Ella wrapped her earasaid around her, tucking her hands among the folds.

An eagle's wailing cry caught her attention, enough to make her narrow her gaze to stare up at the snowfall-covered mountains that ranged ahead and to the right, marching off into the horizon until their softly rounded heads became indiscernible from the sky. The snow line was abrupt. Black pines clambered up the mountains halfway and then stopped as if an invisible barrier was blocking their progress. When Ella looked behind her, she saw the mountains hedged in the loch bay on all sides.

Ella had heard of defensively positioned castles before, but seeing the reality of one in person was very different from learning about them at school, especially living in a country where one-hundred-year-old structures were treated with the same reverence as a monolithic henge.

The manor house was so much more than a medieval building: it was a living, breathing *home*, bustling with activity inside and out and all around. Suddenly, Ella was gripped with a wish to go and see the castle. She wanted to know why no one seemed to be living there and what architectural vision guided the men who were so busy placing the stones and mortaring the corners together.

As she turned to climb back down off the narrow defensive wall, the light beer she had drunk that morning sloshed around in her stomach with a dangerous queasiness. When had she last eaten? Six hundred years ago or six miles back down at the Loch Awe estuary opening into the sea?

"Hie!" She recognized his voice at once. "Will ye nae make it back withoot breakin' yer heid?'

Turning very slowly and carefully so that her hunger had no chance to make her dizzy, Ella shouted her reply down to the captain. "What?"

"Och, Maggie told me you were learning our tongue." He was sitting astride the same horse he had carried her on yesterday, looking up at her with a merry smile. It was as if they had known each other for more than two days. He was wearing another fur cloak around his shoulders, this one was lined in a different color than the one he had given Ella.

"Mither, faither, aye, nay, please, thankee and…ye like. That's about the extent of it." Ella shouted. He beckoned her. "Come down - I will teach you more."

She shook her head. "I can't…I have such hunger! I'm trying to find the kitchens?"

It was a plea and he could not resist it. "Stay. I will come." And with one final wave, Captain Callum pivoted his horse around and galloped out of sight, but Ella guessed he was following the wall back to the gatehouse entrance. She sat down with her back against the stone gable and watched the mist floating into the dell until she heard his approach. He opened the door a fraction and stuck his head around the jamb until he saw her. "If you think I'm going to climb out onto this ledge to get you, lass, you're fair wrong."

What was it about this man? What facet of his personality made Ella feel excited in a way she had never experienced before? Forgetting her hunger, even though it was so acute now that it was painful, Ella stood up to brush her long wool tunic back down around her ankles. "What would you do if I was a damsel in distress, Captain? Would you not come to my rescue?"

He shook his head. "Not if you were wearing that robe, I would not! Honest truth, when Maggie told me she had you dressed as befitting your station, I imagined something more…"

"Something more what?" Ella wanted to know as she took his hand and bent down to pass through the small door again. She jumped off the shallow step and for one moment, they were standing close to one another, holding hands.

"No violent jolt this time?" he asked her with a wry grin. "I do not do it every time apparently," Ella murmured. Then speaking in a louder voice, she demanded he answer her question. "You do not like my tunic?"

"You may think me an innocent lad, lady," he said to her in a mocking voice as he gestured for her to walk down the stone steps in front of him while he held the torch he had placed in the sconce by the doorway, "but I know enough about women not to answer that. I'm regretting the gold I paid me sister to dress you however…a blind forester could cut down a better looking tree."

After filing away the new word in her memory, 'sister,' Ella ignored the jibe and replied without looking back at him. "It might happen that I am perfectly dressed for my station: I am to work in the kitchen. Lady Campbell's orders."

"Och," Callum whistled sharply between his teeth in frustration. "I vow it will nae - not be for long, lass. Auld Col has sent for the priest. He will take his time coming over the mountains, but come he will. Once you're shriven, they cannae hold your ungodly associations against you."

Once they were out of the gloomy stone stairwell that had led Ella up to the rooftop, Callum came to walk beside her, tilting his head over slightly from his greater height to show his interest in what she was saying. "Surely you have a priest closer?" a slight frown creased Ella's brow. "There's an entire castle over yonder hill!" She searched her vocabulary to find the apt phrase to express her impatience. "Must I scrub pots or boil chickens or whatever they order me to do in the kitchen until then…odds bodkins!"

Callum shouted with laughter. When he had vented his mirth, he stopped their progress to interrogate Ella for her choice of words. "You curse like one who has lived on these shores for a goodly while, lass. I believe you are hiding a great deal of your true nature from me."

Ella was feeling surly since hearing the news that she was to go work in the kitchens. "That's rich coming from a man too reluctant to come out onto a rooftop for me," she said in a sulky tone. He heard her and shrugged it off. "You would be reluctant to venture onto roofs too if you were wearing your plaid like a man."

She saw the joke and smiled her usual wide, generous grin. "Again with the plaid? Is the wind up there so biting?"

He winked. "Aye, for some men more than others. Here we are." They had arrived at the kitchen entrance. Ella saw evenly planed stone steps descending into a dark tunnel with not even a sconce to help her see the way in the dark. She held out her hand toward Callum. "May I take the torch? If I must work for my bread, I pray they give it to me first before they ask for the work! I am famished!"

Callum stepped closer but held the torch too high for her to reach. "Would you care to share my food with me? I have plenty in my saddlebags. My duty is to ride down to the loch to check if the stone masons have quarried enough ballast to tide them over until the Lord's Day. Why not come?"

"Why not indeed?" Instead of walking down to the kitchens, Ella placed her hand on Callum's elbow, accepting his escort to the stables.

This time, the surge of electricity was weaker, as if she had been walking along a long hotel corridor and then touched the doorknob of her hotel room rather than sticking her finger in a plug socket. Callum felt it too but said nothing.

Chapter 7

Callum handed her a bannock from the saddlebag before throwing her into the saddle sideways. Adjusting her posture with strong hands, he showed Ella how to sit sideways, with one thigh poised on top of the horse's withers and the other thigh inside the saddle with the pommel pushing up between her legs.

While holding her legs in those positions as he grasped the halter firmly to keep the horse still, Callum touched her in a neutral manner which let Ella know that while she might be ready to ride to the other side of the hill with him, she was in safe hands. When he could feel she was as comfortable as she was ever going to get, he mounted behind her, keeping a-hold of the reins in one hand, reaching around to stroke the horse's neck with his other hand, keeping her pressed tightly between his arms.

Ella felt him smile as she gobbled the bannock. She could taste oats and honey, and something very like lard or butter mixed into the heavy pastry. The bannocks were light and crunchy, and Ella took a flying guess that she would not be eating such high-quality breakfast when she was a scullion maid in the kitchens!

Riding with the saddle's pommel tucked between her legs felt strange for a while, especially with one hand holding the bannock and her bottom hanging off the opposite side to her legs for balance, but Ella adapted to the pose quickly.

She searched for the French word for intimate in her mind, but could not remember it. Ella decided to settle for using the word '*proche*' for closeness. "It is a close way to travel," she remarked in a light tone as they retraced their tracks from yesterday, only this time at a brisk trot. She wanted to ask him if he had ever ridden with another woman in front of him, but was too shy. He seemed to be thinking about his answer.

"It is not likely that you will be able to travel any other way unless you like to walk. Do you dislike it?"

Ella searched for the right words to say, deeply regretting the way she could not be spontaneous and witty. Back in Glenorchy, New Zealand, Ella had been a hit with most of the single guys in the region, but Ella had an inkling that was only because of online digital photoshopping that made her look like a cat and the application of lots of mascara in real life; they never made much of a push to come to Glenorchy to meet her in person.

Ella hated the thought of this man seeing her fair eyelashes in all their unadorned glory. She must look like a white rabbit.

It's the same feeling as opening the door to a visitor when you least expect it and finding the man of your dreams standing in front of you and you had no time to prepare.

Giving up, she replied. "I like it very much. Tell me how to say that in your language."

"*J'aime bien ou j'aime?*" Callum asked her.

Ella knew that the French word for love and like were the same. I love: I like. The only way the French could quantify the word was to add the word 'bien' - that one little word changed love to like in a flash. Callum had asked her to quantify its meaning; did she want to learn the word for love or like?

If Ella said '*j'aime bien*' that would mean she had wanted to say 'I like it well enough.' If she stuck to her original phrase, Callum was at liberty to take her words to mean that she loved riding with him in the way that they were.

Finally, she hit upon a compromise. "Tell me how to say I love it *and* I like it. Do you not agree that those words are *equally* important ones to learn?"

She felt laughter rumbling in his chest. "Aye, lass. They are. If you are quite finished, may I suggest you shake the crumbs off your tunic afore we arrive at the castle?" Callum reached to one side of the saddle and Ella could not stop herself from giving a little scream as she felt off balance.

Immediately, Callum reassured her and steadied her with his hand. "I'm getting you some mead to wash down the bannock. It will be nice to not thirst now that you have no hunger, not so?"

"Give me some warning next time you do that if it is your will." She had used the Scots expression for please: if it is your will.

He was silent for a short while, looking at the workmen's progress as they approached the castle walls. After halting, it seemed to Ella that he gave her waist a light squeeze before he said, "You please me greatly when you speak my tongue, lass."

Callum dismounted next to a water trench with a post beside it and began twisting the halter around the post. "But that is how a child or a lowly person makes their request," he continued, glancing up at her to watch her reaction. "Is this how you wish to address me?" He held out his arms for her to jump into.

Ella jumped, and when he set her down steady on her feet, she replied in a calm voice. "Let's wait to see what the priest says about me before I start getting ideas above my station." She had noticed the way he had gone from calling her 'lady' to calling her 'lasse'. It meant that Callum saw her as a maiden or a young girl, not a respectful matron. She tried not to be so pleased about this but failed. It thrilled Ella to her core to be Callum's lass.

She had to admire his shrewd assessment of how she felt about going to work in the kitchens though. A small and very modern part of her was beginning to feel irritated with her new situation. Yes, she was grateful to be alive and ecstatic to be trapped in such a beautiful part of the world, but no amount of blue skies and black loch waters would make up for the fact that she was really meant to be a young girl enjoying her final teenage year touring interesting places with a fair amount of spare cash stashed on her bank cards.

Her fingers felt empty without a phone to hold, and her mind felt blank without her books. Ella was wearing a hand-stitched band of homespun wool attached to her shapeless tunic hem instead of comfortable lycra-assisted denim legging jeans. The pointed toes and downtrodden backs of the scuffed and crusty leather poulaines on her feet flapped and slapped the flagstones like clown shoes whenever she took a step, and her mascara! Dear God, how was she to live without mascara? How did people live without mirrors in their rooms? And books on their bedside tables?

"Will you accompany me?" Callum spoke to her over his shoulder, breaking off from speaking to the mason who had come out of the main entrance of the castle to speak with him.

"Aye, aye," Ella pushed the soft wooden peg back into the neck of the leather pouch of mead and placed it back into the saddlebag. The firkin's neck had been hardened with a resinous substance and then tied with a thin cord to make it fit the wooden peg; the leather pouch was airtight. After inspecting the firkin closely, Ella was amazed at how handy and perfectly suited for its purpose the firkin was. Maybe she would not miss plastic so much after all.

Ella soon got bored of watching the castle from the outside; she wanted to go inside and look around. And she wanted Callum to be her guide when she did it.

So newly out of her early and mid-teen years, Ella recognized the blossoming emotions of hero worship for the man standing in front of her. Edging around the water trough to be able to look at Callum more closely, she could observe him from under her eyelashes without him thinking it forward of her.

He was the type of man no woman would ever tire of looking at. Ella judged the captain's age to be somewhere in his early twenties. His high-cut cheekbones were smooth, showing no sign of stray hairs or encroaching hirsuteness that a man in his thirties or forties would have. Callum was semi-clean shaven; as a soldier who had obviously been out patrolling, living off the land had every right to be. Red stubble darkened his angular jawline and determined chin.

He bent his head to listen closely to the story the mason was telling him, rubbing one hand along his cheek as if remembering he had not scraped the beard stubble off his face that morning. Ella realized that seeing her on top of the manor's walls that morning must have taken Callum unawares, and he had reacted on the spur of the moment with his invitation to show her around. She liked that. She liked the fact that he was the kind of man who did not care to shave meticulously every morning. Somehow it suited him.

The red of Callum's beard was echoed by the myriad of russet shades in his hair. It was a riveting color, with dark red locks clustering rather wildly around his face to frame it, but the hair grew lighter the further away it got from the crown until the waves were almost red-gold at the nape of his neck.

It was not only Callum's hair and face that were eye-catching. His shoulders joined the neck by way of two impressive trapezius muscles; his deltoids, biceps, triceps, and every other arm 'cep Ella cared to remember from her high school biology curriculum were not only

66

extremely bulky but also well-defined. The captain's legs would make a man think twice before attempting to tackle him to the ground. When added to the layer his winter clothing provided him, Callum Campbell was an intimidating size even though his hips and waist were still slim with youth.

His nose was manly, aquiline, rising like a hatchet to give him a haughty look when he turned to profile. Callum's nose almost gave him a dangerous appearance, like a man who had vengeance and battle on his mind. Wherever Ella looked at him, she was reminded of the ruthless way he had attacked and slain the Bonawe isle brigands...and how he had not so much as batted an eye in regret afterward.

But then he would smile, which had the power to make his pure blue eyes sparkle in a fatally alluring way.

This being the middle ages, Callum, why aren't you married? Your sister Margaret is about to be betrothed and she's only twelve! Maybe you are married...and you're hiding some fabulously sad story about a wife who died in childbirth, because surely no wife would allow her husband to go trotting around the countryside with a young woman who had to ride with his saddle pommel thrusting between her thighs!

It was as if he could hear her thoughts out loud. Suddenly, Callum's intensely blue stare turned on her and he frowned. Ella could not help herself - she held her breath.

"I am being impolite, lass," he said, stepping close to where she stood and taking her hand. "But I had reason. My uncle-" he used the Scots word for this appellation and nodded when Ella showed she was following what he was saying, "-Colin is impatient to return to his castle."

"Is there something wrong with the castle?" Ella took a shot in the dark with her question, hoping to distract him from whatever had made him turn to look at her.

He guided her toward the entrance. "Aye. We were forced to lower the flag and set up in the auld manor house over two years ago. You cannot see it now - at high tide - but the causeway collapsed, thus rendering our access impossible after the stone stairs fell into disrepair soon after."

As their progress grew closer to the loch, Ella was able to see that what she had first thought to be a pile of stones waiting to be mortared into place was actually a failed staircase. Well, maybe the staircase was too luxurious a term for the steep incline of steps that joined the small entrance in the castle's second or third floor. There were no handrails, no landing, and no newels. Even as a visitor here with permission of Sir Colin's nephew, Ella found that the steep, narrow ledge jutting out from the wall had a forbidding aspect.

"Is that it?" she asked in a less than medieval tone of voice. "Is that the only way to get to the castle? A broken causeway and a doorway even I would struggle to get through?"

Ella craned her neck to look up at the crenellations on the stone tower, shaking her head and tutting. She knew that castles were meant to be impenetrable, but this was ridiculous!

"What would you do?" Callum was as perplexed by her questions as Ella was by the complete lack of entrances and exits. "It is a defensible position. Sir Colin and his lady spent twenty years on its completion. It is a sturdy keep - dinnae let the failed steps tell ye otherwise, not that I expect a lass to understand."

He muttered the last words under his breath, but Ella was able to guess their meaning. "Forgive me, Captain Callum. The manor house made me think there would be stables and a courtyard and a formal garden - in fact, all those things that make a house a home."

He chuckled, forgiving her immediately. "Och lass, you will like the place well enough when we are under attack. As for stables and gardens and whatnot, that's what the manor house is for. We maintain our fields for harvesting and grazing along the River Orchy. Within easy marching distance of the keep."

Ella had nothing to say about what it must be like to have to live within marching distance of an impregnable castle keep in case of an attack and began to better understand why the Campbells had set about eliminating the brigands.

Taking her hand and leading her to a vantage point where Ella could watch the masons' apprentices wading in the loch trying to spear a fish for supper, elevated above the freezing water by strange-looking wooden chopines, Callum explained the lay of the land to her.

"You can see the approach of ships coming up the River Awe and Loch Awe from the western tower. The trick is this: vessels cannot sail close enough because of the shallow waters. And if they try attacking on foot this way, we can cut the causeway rope slats and they will sink into the mire." Pulling Ella to another spot, Callum continued explaining the castle's strategic defenses. "The only way inside was by going up and down the stone steps. You would have laughed to see the ladies' faces on the morning they woke up and noticed the steps were disappeared! We had to carry them down by rope as we had no ladder long enough!"

That did make Ella laugh. She could not imagine the prim and whey-faced Lady Campbell clambering down a rope thrown through her bedchamber window! "Were you not also marooned in such a fashion?" she asked.

Callum shook his head. "Nay. I stay at the manor house barracks when my commander is away."

"Are you not the one to command Sir Colin's soldiers?" Ella was surprised. Callum had the air of someone who was born to command.

"I live under the command of Duncan, Sir Colin and Lady Margaret's eldest son. He is away at court at this time."

How convenient for Duncan to be prancing around at the King's court while his cousin sorts out the brigands for him.

Ella kept this dry observation to herself.

"The stonemason has good news." Callum gave Ella's hand a squeeze as he smiled. "The foundations have been laid. I can send for the wood wright to build the treadwheel. This should interest you - Sir Colin has been known to send servants to tread the wheel."

"Are those my choices," Ella joked, "scrubbing pots or treading the wheel?"

"Aye," Callum said in a more off-hand tone than he had used before. "At least they are until you are shriven. Once the sin of your association with those diabhal worshiping brigands has been removed from your soul, you can begin to look about you for a husband."

He used the French words 'votre bon homme,' which Ella did not entirely understand. "'My own good man'? I don't...?"

"Mo dhuine, lass. That is what our womenfolk call their husbands in our tongue." He used the French word this time: mari.

Blushing a furious red, which Ella needed no mirror to tell her was happening because she could feel her cheeks were on fire, Ella dropped Callum's hand and walked away to the loch shore, waiting for her blushes to fade.

Breathing deeply, Ella tried not to panic. Her new life had become inconceivably complicated in such a short time. Once again, she yearned for the life that she had been born into. A life where she could take Callum by the hand and lead him over to some summery, sun-dappled copse of trees, where they might lie down together and chat about taking their relationship to the next level. Where a kiss would not get her burned at the stake and fornication would not get her offending orifice stretched out by the Pear of Anguish.

She felt him approach after a while. "Why do you shy like a mare who distrusts the halter? Is someone waiting for you back at your home?" He no longer stood beside her. Instead, Callum moved to stand behind her while he waited to know her mind.

That was a question that Ella might answer with a thousand words or none at all. All at once, the fumbling embraces of her first high school boyfriend flashed into her mind. The rude way he had thrust his thick tongue into her mouth as if he was trying to push her away instead of trying to coax her closer.

With her senior year boyfriend; they had gone five years of high school and attended classes together until deciding to make out at a weekend party they both happened to be attending. It had run its course by the time Ella decided to stay in Glenorchy instead of moving to Nelson to attend a tech school there. Yes, they had attempted to 'do it' and 'go all the way,' but he had no condoms on hand and Ella had been too afraid of falling pregnant. She remembered the tentative way they had gone about relieving themselves and tried to suppress a smile. It was no surprise that she was still a virgin when she had always preferred reading about making love instead of actually doing it.

For Ella, love and intimacy were all about Heathcliff and Cathy; Tristan and Isolde; Mr. Rochester and Jane Eyre; Scarlett and Rhett. Those books gave her the best glimpse of how she wanted her love life to be one day. Yes, she knew - all too well - that making love was all about strange scents and tastes as saliva and sharply inhaled breaths collided. Gooey bodily fluids and embarrassing grunts and squeaks as bodies slid up and down against one another and the sweat caused the slick skin to suction together with a wet squelch. So, it was no wonder that she could say to this man now -

"I have no one, Callum…no one."

Overlooking that icy, iron-gray loch with its frost burnt shores and lowering clouds, Ella experienced true despair for the first time in her cosseted twenty-first-century existence. If she stayed here, she would have to act contrary to her nature forever. Be a maiden on her wedding night, go on to be a good wife, birth children with no pain management or doula or baby-centric websites, and cross her fingers she didn't die in the process. And if she enjoyed her husband's touch too much, it would be a hit-or-miss wish that a baby did not follow forty weeks later.

One sorrowful eagle cry high above her was all it took for Ella to dissolve into tears. She was all alone in space and time as the two centuries inside her collided.

She saw his hands rest gently on her shoulders before Callum pulled her close to his chest and wrapped his arms around her waist. She felt his breath warm the top of her head as his mouth rested on the top of her cap there.

They stood together at the edge of the loch like that for what seemed like a long while before he broke their silence.

"I have heard tell of lassies with hair as pale as yours; how they are hunted and coveted and sold like the most precious jewels. Is it true that yellow-haired women are kept in cages, waiting for their hair to be harvested every ten years?"

Ella grasped at anything that would take her mind off her emotional pain. "Yes - aye, at least they used to do such things when Romans roamed this land - for hair to make wigs."

He hugged her tighter, growling with humor. "The Romans never dared to come here for their hair, lass!"

That made her laugh and brush away her tears after knuckling her eyes with both hands. "You are right - and I am being foolish. Forgive me for these girlish megrims."

Still, within the circle of his arms, Ella turned to thank Callum. He had come to her rescue in so many ways since she first met him that Ella was quite happy to believe in brave knights rescuing damsels in distress.

Her face was uptilted; his face was bent down. It was the most natural thing in the world for Callum and Ella to kiss. At first, the only thing Ella was aware of was the way his beard stubble pricked her skin. The rough texture was almost too dominating for her to think of anything else. But gradually she relaxed and allowed herself to enjoy this new sensation. The pressure he was using to kiss her was firm, yet yielding. Ella felt softly female underneath the touch of his mouth, and she could not stop herself from responding with quickened breath and a small sigh escaping as she exhaled.

And then it was over. He seemed to be judging her reaction as he continued to stare down at her.

"Ye're a bonny lass, Ella Campbell." He spoke in his own language.

Catching his hand to her mouth, Ella kissed his palm in a frenzy of gratitude and ardent attraction, her thoughts were too jumbled to think about what she wanted to thank Callum for; all she knew was that his kiss had the power to lighten her sorrow.

"Hie! Leave some o' that sweet morsel for me!" The cheerful bellow echoed off the castle walls and surrounding hills and made Ella drop Callum's hand like it was a bannock straight out of the fire grate.

She saw a faint flutter of irritation cross Callum's face and could identify with the emotion. If she had to be stuck here in mid-fifteenth-century Scotland, the one thing that might brighten her bleak existence would be having Captain Callum Campbell as her boyfriend.

They both turned around to watch the small group of horsemen trotting toward them, and so Ella was treated to her first sight of proper medieval splendor and grandeur. And the first thing that caught her eye was the charmstone amulet fastened to the jacket worn by the man at the head of the riders.

Chapter 8

There was no doubt the rider's amulet was a match for the charmstone now hanging around her neck. For one moment, Ella felt like hiding behind Callum's tall form and peeking out at the man when he would not be aware of her gaze. But that time was past: the man was aware of her and seemed to be looking at her with a greedy gaze.

"Cousin, this is the slave girl and chattel to the brigands yer faither must have told ye aboot." Callum translated the words he said for Ella to understand. She promptly tried to memorize as many of the words as possible. Cousin; slave girl; chattel. She already knew 'faither'.

"Aye, I have come here straight from his side," the man said, "I find the court to be a dreary place in winter. Hollyrood is so cold I swear the choir's songs froze in the air before they could reach the ear! Still, the trip was not without merit. His majesty's disgruntlement at being crowned at Holyrood instead of Scone seems to have simmered down. You say the girl speaks French?" The man's eyes raked Ella up and down. "How…courteous of her." The words were said with a sneer, which was immediately replaced by a leer as the wind whipped Ella's tunic closer to her body. "Is she sweet?"

He said the words in French for Ella to understand: Est-elle doux?

Ella wanted to smack the arrogant man's face, if not for his lecherous expression than for his preposterous clothes. The rich, thick, red velvet doublet he was wearing had gold threads tacked through the puffed top sleeves, made to hang down but now blowing in the late morning winter breeze. The doublet was short enough for Ella to see the white linen chemise he was wearing tucked under his hose, barely hidden by the silk pouch codpiece. As for the parti-colored hose tied to the man's waistband, one was blue and the other was maroon; these leggings were themselves tucked into a splendid pair of red leather poulaines with toe points hanging over the stirrups like two melted pizza slices. The doublet had a thick seam of velvet around its waist-line, where gold threads also fluttered, some of which had been used to keep the hose high. A flaring piece of skirt frilled out from the doublet's waistline, stopping well short of his mid-thigh. A gray sideless mantle cape was thrown over both shoulders; a wide-brimmed fur cap completed the ensemble.

Callum did not answer the question and Ella was too aware of the slight tension in the air to try and see what expression was on his face. All she knew was that the captain had not answered the man's question as to whether she was sweet or not.

The rider circled his hand in the air, directing the gesture toward Ella and telling Callum, "Make me known to her. Make our introduction."

Ella knew what he was saying. The man's French was eloquent and perfect, not like the halting and hesitant phrases Callum and she spoke to one another.

"Cousin Duncan, this maiden claims the name of Ella Campbell. Ella, Duncan Campbell, the firstborn son of Sir Colin, is kind enough to make himself known to you."

Duncan placed his gloved hand on his heart and waited for Ella to tell him how honored she was to meet him. Callum helped her along by subtly poking her in the back.

"Charmed, I'm sure," was all the enthusiasm Ella could muster up. The wilting sarcasm was lost on Duncan. "I am pleased with you, girl," he announced to the men behind him, giving them a little wink. "Come. Accompany me back to our manor house. I wish to hear a recount of your adventures."

Ella noticed that Duncan used the thee and thou pronouns when he was talking to her. In medieval Scotland - and everywhere else in England and Europe for that matter - 'thee and thou' was generally used to address social inferiors or children while 'ye' was used when talking to equals, family, and loved ones. Callum had addressed her using 'ye' from the first time they spoke to one another in French...

No, you don't wish to hear about my adventures. I am willing to bet I caught your eye when you saw me kissing your Cousin Callum's palm back there.

But all Ella said out loud was, "Och aye."

This casual acquiescence to Duncan's magnanimous offer made the riders surrounding Duncan break out laughing. "She speaks our tongue. Go careful with this great scholar!"

Ella wanted to keep an eye on the charmstone attached so casually to the man's doublet. She had no plan in mind, she only wanted to see if 'Cousin Duncan' treated the amulet like a treasure or another piece of jewelry.

Waving his entourage away with one languid hand as he ordered one of his men to give up his horse for Ella to ride, she raised her voice. "Alas, I cannot ride alone. My slavemasters never taught me."

Duncan looked at her with a crafty frown marring his brow. "Then how did you arrive at the castle this morn?"

There was no way Ella was going to tell this man the truth. She was already regretting her cocksure agreement to converse with this man, away from Callum's protective guidance. "By my own means, sir. I am resourceful and lucky. Two precious traits to have if one is a slave." She hoped that Callum did not contradict her.

Amazingly, her answer seemed to both please and placate Duncan. "Very well. You may sit behind me as we ride back. It is quite safe. And need I to mention that it is also a great honor? You are a kitchen scullion, after all, at least until the priest shrives thee."

Ella gave one last lingering look back at Callum, but he had already untied the halter from the post and was mounting his horse. Trying hard not to hate Duncan for separating her from the captain only moments after their first kiss, Ella concentrated on giving Sir Colin's eldest son a good impression of herself.

After accepting his hand and lifting herself up onto the back of the saddle, gingerly placing her hands around Duncan's waist and suppressing her surprise when most of his impressive build turned out to be padding stuffed into the doublet seams, Ella settled down to answer Callum's cousin's questions.

"Tell me all your story," Duncan raised his voice so that Ella might hear his command even as the wind picked it up and whisked it away across the loch.

Thanking her lucky stars that she had read countless story books, Ella began.

My mither died before I was old enough to remember her. I was raised by a slave woman. She spoke the language of the Ural Mountains, those folks with flat cheekbones and strangely slanted, dark gray eyes. The people with nostrils that flare like a horse when it whinnies with fear and paws the ground with its hooves. Her wide smile is the first thing I can remember.

I was taught to fetch and carry and finish my chores just like every other child of the Norse. Only later did I realize that my work was done in bondage. I was a silent child out of habit. There were many slaves from many parts of the world all in one camp. We spoke a mix of sign language and Latin. This was good because I was able to pick up French very quickly once I was surrounded by the language.

My Ural foster-mither told me what she knew about my real mither before the sweet lady died. Maybe she was married to my faither, maybe not - who's to say? After saying a tearful farewell to my Ural foster-mither, I took the name Campbell with me to my new home: a French merchant's house in the port town of Bergen.

Not long ago, I strayed too far down the coast while searching for cockles. After rounding one bend, I saw the brigands' sloop anchored in the shallow waters, as such vessels are able to do. The brigands were filling their urns with fresh water on the shore and gave me chase, and captured me.

There was some bickering over whether they should ravish me or keep me whole for sale. I understood parts of the argument. Until they decided on my fate, I was made to keep the fires burning for them and cook their food. They permitted me to use the bay to wash. I was planning to try and escape but...

Then Callum came.

"You tell your story true and well," was Duncan's quick opinion. "I have heard that the folk from those far-off mountains can tell stories around the campfire that last all night. Is that true?"

"I believe so, sir, although a slave would hardly have the stamina to do such a thing." Ella felt Duncan shift angrily in the saddle and attempted to change the subject before he could scold her. "I see you have a charm stone on your beautiful cote. Did you get it in Holyrood?"

For some strange reason, Duncan seemed reluctant to talk about the amulet. He continued as though Ella had not even spoken.

"When our bard returns in spring, you must speak with him. Perhaps he and ye might sing the sad story of your life together at the summer solstice feast?"

"Is he the same bard who wrote The Brus?" the question popped out before Ella could stop herself. Almost, just almost, she stopped herself from clapping a hand over her mouth which would have compounded her suspicious statement double-fold. Duncan sounded peevish when he said. "Bard John Barbour is dead these fifty years ago now. Where heard ye about our ballad of The Brus?"

Ella dissembled. "Er…a traveling bard in the north…" The moment the ostler ran out to help Duncan out of his horse, Ella slithered down the animal's hindquarters and ran toward the manor side entrance Callum had shown her to yesterday, shouting behind her. "Thankee for returning me here, sir, thankee. Farewell."

Ella needed time alone to think about the amulet Duncan Campbell had been wearing, and she had no desire to be questioned more closely about her miraculous ability to know about Scottish ballads while living in Scandinavia.

"Halt!" An evil-looking poleaxe with a cruel hook on one side of the axe sliced in front of Ella's nose. She lost all pretense of being a runaway slave in the Middle Ages, the shock of nearly becoming hideously maimed was all she could think about. "Jesus! You nearly cut off my nose, you oaf! How dare you!" Stepping back from the guard who had shot the poleaxe across the doorway to stop her entering, Ella screamed with rage. It was too much: she was not some scared and biddable servant - she was the daughter of a successful retail magnate and his genius website developer wife, granddaughter of Gran Campbell who was more Scottish than these prancing ninnies and ignorant barbarians could ever wish to be…and here they were slicing axes in front of her face, missing her nose by a hairsbreadth! Ella had not counted all the accumulated wealth her parents had left in trust for her, but she held the notion that it would be enough to buy this crappy manor house and most of the land around it too.

"How dare you - *how dare you* - how freaking *dare* you!" Now that she had started, she could not stop. Ella screamed the words, stamping her feet in a dance of fury and punching the air with her fists. The words that were now bubbling out of her mouth had been knocking on the door of her emotions since her head had broken out of the water yesterday morning. The helpless confusion and shock churned around her head and blocked out all survival instincts and restraint. All Ella could think of was that she did not belong here in this nightmare.

"Ella!" Callum's voice broke through the red mist of rage. "What diabhal has taken hold of you?" But not even the deep concern in his voice was enough to calm Ella down. She continued to scream and stamp, venting her frustration and horror at her incomprehensible predicament. Not even when she heard Callum rage at his cousin in French. "What did you say to the girl? What did you do?"

Cousin Duncan took umbrage at the accusation. "She was off the horse and running inside before I could do anything! I mean…that is to say…I would never touch a hair on her head!"

Callum went to the guard, picking him up by his leather cuirass sleeve holes and shaking the man mercilessly. "You knave. Did you hurt the lady? Tell me now before I knock it out of you!" Through her tantrum, Ella could see that Callum was on her side and it went a long way to help her calm down. She began to gulp down the air, bending forward to put her hands on her knees as she caught her breath. She hoped that Callum would kill the man. The guard's action would have decapitated her if she had been shorter.

"Nay, sir, on my life. I am only following your orders! You yourself trained me to slam the halberd across the doorway and into the wood frame!" Here, the man pointed to the wooden door frame opposite his post, as if to prove his point. The wood was indeed scarred with hews that matched the halberd's edge. Ella knew what the two men were talking about because they were saying halberd. Ella had never bothered to learn the exact differences between the weapons, but it was comforting to know that Callum was on her side.

"Callum," Ella raised her voice, holding out one hand, palm facing toward him. "Forgive me. Let the man go. Please tell me the door I may use to access my bedchamber."

Ella wanted to go and lie down. No way was she going to work in the kitchen. She must find a way to fix this mess and get back to her time and place in this crazy, mixed-up universe. Callum did not respond to her question at once, leaving it up to his cousin to fill in for him, which Duncan seemed very willing to do. "Alack, girl, my mither has not yet assigned you a cot, and you can hardly stay in Margaret's bedchamber, you understand - you are lately a slave! As pleased as I am to see that your fit has dissipated, I must advise my cousin to house you in the cellars - only until the priest has come to check for diabhals-" Duncan saw Ella's shocked reaction to his statement and must have been fearful of her falling down into another fit. "You have my word that a cot will be provided for you once Faither Archibald the priest has inspected you."

Anything was better than slaving in the kitchens as far as Ella was concerned, but she caught the look of concern in Callum's eyes and hoped it was related to something else.

"Come," Duncan held out his hand toward Ella. "Promise to be a good girl and I will demean myself by showing you to the cellars myself." He turned to Callum. "Where is the key?"

Ella did not understand the cousins' conversation, but she could follow enough to know that an argument ensued. It was an argument that Callum won, however. Duncan stomped off back to the stables and Callum dragged her by the hand inside the door, growling something to the guard who said nothing back, only made a low bow to his captain.

"Have you lost your mind?" Callum was as close to exasperation as such a rock-steady man could be. "Did the diabhal take hold of your soul?"

"Fermez la bouche!" Ella muttered. She had been wanting to tell the two cousins to shut up for a while now, but only saying it to Callum was good enough. He dropped her hand once they were passed the heavy tapestries that guarded the hall entrance so that he could turn around and face her. "What did you say to me!?" Ella did not answer but had the wisdom to hang her head with a shamefaced expression to show her contrition. Giving an exasperated sigh, Callum took hold of her hand again, leading her down a dank passage after removing a torch from the wall sconce and lighting it in the alcove fire.

They reached a heavy wooden door, studded all over with embossments, the wood decorated with black curlicues from a hot poker. Attached to a cumbersome latch that bolted the door was a crude lock.

"Welcome to your new bedchamber," Callum informed her, his lips pressed together in a grim line. "Are you satisfied now? Duncan has deemed you too unruly to be housed with the clan."

On those words, Callum lifted a chunky key out of the fur and leather pouch belted around his waist and inserted it into the lock. He pushed the door open, using all of his strength and shoving with his shoulders. The hinges protested and squeaked, reminding Ella of every horror movie soundtrack she had ever heard.

He held Ella back when she tried to look inside. "Wait, you will need light." Going down the steps ahead of her, Callum ordered her to stay on the threshold. Ella could see nothing but the blinding light of the torch flame dancing ever downwards. "What's down there?" she shouted after Callum's retreating back.

His voice sounded dull as the deep, rich accent of his words was swallowed by the starkly frigid air. "Vittles and wine. It's the cellar." He stepped aside, out of Ella's line of sight so that she would not be blinded as she came down. When she reached the bottom, Callum placed the torch into a wall sconce so she could look around.

The cellar was vast in length, but the roughly hewn ceiling was so low Callum had to stoop his neck forward. As her eyes grew used to the dimness, Ella saw heaps of turnips piled up in woven baskets, crates of leeks, roughly made chests full of wrinkled apples, and withered peas still in the pod. Jute sacks were stuffed full of round bobbles of shelled beans, and dozens of barrels lined the walls and floor. The smell of barley and wheat grain seeped out of the barrels.

"I cannot stay here," Ella could hardly speak, her teeth were already chattering. "This will kill me." With no fire grate and no cot, not even the wolf pelt cloak and earasaid could protect Ella from the cold. "I should go back to the kitchens," Ella suggested as she rubbed her upper arms with her hands after pulling the woolen shawl over her head. "They have fires there."

Callum took pity on her. "I will leave the torch for you. The bell sounded for dinner some time back. I will return here with some food for you after dining with my uncle. I hope to bend his ear into giving you better sleeping quarters. He does not listen to Duncan but makes up his own mind on things."

The full consequences of her tantrum were dawning on Ella. Fear of being left alone in a freezing cellar made her bold. Running up to Callum, she threw herself against him, wrapping her arms around his waist tightly before tilting her face up to plead with him. "Do not leave me here to die of cold, Callum, I'm begging you. I *know* you feel the bond we have; it is that link that brought us together. Take me to the kitchens, please! I will work hard, I swear."

He tried to remove her grip on him, but she shook her head and held on tighter. "The foutering diabhal has got nothing to do with my fit - I was frightened by the guard's axe. You must believe me, Callum!"

For that moment, it felt to Ella as if she was hugging a tall pine tree on one of the mountains that surrounded the castle for all the response she got from Callum, and then he relented. "Och lass, you must stop saying such things. Only God may propose the future."

The statement made Ella laugh wildly, but she insisted he answer her before she let go. "Take me to the kitchens, Callum. I'll be good."

"Verra well," he said in Scots Gaelic, shaking his head at the way this young woman was able to wrap him around her finger in such a short time of knowing her. "Was that yes?" Ella insisted on knowing. Sighing, he lifted the torch off the sconce and walked to the steps after removing Ella's hand from his waist to lead her back into the light. "It is the same as *très bien*. Ella, there is a reason why I was happy to lock you in the cellars…Duncan is not a…*restrained* man. You have no one to protect you if he should take it into his head to woo you. Listen not to his blandishments, lass, no matter how much he tries to tempt you. Duncan is betrothed to another."

"Yes, yes," Ella was relieved to be leaving the cellar behind with every step and was not at all interested in becoming Mrs. Duncan Campbell now or ever.

But Callum was not finished with his warnings. "I will tell the cook - Martha - that you are a deaf-mute serving girl come to form part of me sister's entourage, but Margaret has no use for you." He placed his hands over his ears and mouth in case Ella did not understand the new role she was to play. "Complete all the tasks Cook sets you to do, and do not forget the role you must play. Keep your hair tied under the scarf in case word of your appearance has spread. And whatever you do, lass, never leave your new lodgings until I tell you it is safe."

They were at the passage entrance, which was empty because all the household were dining in the hall and every servant off duty was eating in the kitchen. "If I treat you rough in front of the Cook, Ella, forgive me. Expect no special treatment when others are watching…it might stick a spoke in the wheel of your progress."

Callum was about to step down into the kitchen stairwell, but Ella stopped him. "I cannot thank you enough, Captain. Your chivalry and bravery is unmatched."

He froze, and Ella thought for one moment that her words of praise were unwelcome, but then he crushed her to his chest, muttering his strange language as he kissed the top of her head. Even through the thick earasaid wool and linen cap, she could feel the heat of his breath as he whispered the words that she so badly wanted to understand.

Standing on tiptoes, Ella did what she had been wanting to do ever since she had seen him call up to her on the roof that morning: she wrapped her arms around his neck and pulled his face down to meet her kiss. Tempted by the fact that he would not be able to understand a word she said, Ella could not resist telling him. "I think I love you, Callum Campbell."

Recognizing his name, the captain smiled as he kissed her, their mouths slotting into one another's so perfectly that it felt like they had become an extension of one instead of two separate entities.

And for the first time in her life, Ella admitted to herself with no hesitation that she was in love, and this was what love felt like to fall truly, madly, deeply in love, almost at first sight. This was not just a physical realization, but a metaphysical one. Would she move heaven and earth to stay here with Callum for the rest of her life?

Maybe that was no longer a question she had to answer.

Chapter 9

It was the memory of that kiss that sustained Ella over the next four days. Reminding herself of every affirmation and 10 Rules to Succeed in Life self-improvement book she had ever read, somehow Ella was able to maintain her image as deaf-mute; someone who could think of nothing better to do than wake up at what felt like two o'clock in the morning every day and slave herself to the bone until well past sundown.

Yes, she knew the nights felt long and the days felt short because it was winter, but once she became more familiar with her surroundings, Ella was able to gauge there were around six hours of gray daylight during the day, followed by an hour after hour of black night.

She was allowed to lay her weary head down on a straw bolster by the fire pit to sleep, but only after every pot had been scrubbed clean with sand and every glass goblet had been washed fingerprint free with boiling water and ash lye. The Cook would kick her awake at around four in the morning before lumping back to her warm bed after ordering Ella to spark the fires and set the cauldrons to boil. Not long after, the scullions would enter to lift the massive cauldrons out of the fire pit with special iron rods and carry them over to the spit roast hearth. There, they would throw oats and salt into the water to make the servants porridge to break their fast.

Only when the warm smell of porridge had filled the lower level of the manor house did the servants begin to trickle inside, yawning and scratching, to sit down in the servants' parlor - the room where they were able to speak freely without punishment from the Cook who demanded they work at all hours - to eat the porridge that Ella had served and to drink the small beer that Ella had brought up from the alehouse the previous evening and warmed by the fire in between stirring the porridge.

For that was how it went in great houses and castles during the Middle Ages: the last servant to be hired became servant to all the others.

Ella did not mind the hard work, because at least it kept her mind busy. If she had a few moments to herself during the day, memories of Callum and his kiss rushed in to haunt her. At night, if she had not been so exhausted, it would have been the same. He had not returned to check on her or to tell her that the flood of love that had swept over her during their kiss was the feeling he had for her too.

This was real life, hard as it was to believe, not one of Ella's romantic tales. It reminded Ella of her first crush.

She had been invited to a party in Queenstown and Gran Campbell had permitted her to go if her granddaughter could sleep over at her friend's house. Ella had been thirteen, he had been fifteen. They had danced together, chatted together, and then moved to the patio to canoodle and make out. At the end of the evening. Ella had given him the gift shop phone number, which he had dutifully entered into his phone, and then they had kissed each other goodnight, promising to meet again the following weekend in Queenstown.

"What time should we meet?" Ella had been anxious to know. "Let's meet at Burger King, but what time? If my Gran answers the phone, just hang up - what time are you going to call?" She had peppered him with questions, desperate to lock him into a commitment so she could go to school the next day and tell her girlfriends about her new boyfriend who was so hot and cute.

But he had never called or turned up at the Burger King. Ella had spent an entire month hanging out at the gift shop and jumping to answer the phone when it rang, only to have her hopes dashed every time. By the time the fifth week came around, her sulking made Gran Campbell agree to get her a phone so that Ella would never have to go through the humiliation of being ghosted again.

And yet here she was again. Sighing and waiting for a man who had turned her world upside down. When she had time, Ella would go and sit with Oswald the spit-turn boy, and point at things with a raised brow so he would tell her what the word was for it in Scots. They would take a pull at their large tankards of small beer and she would wipe her mouth with the back of her hand while listening to him chatter. Oswald was a victim of the rigid hierarchical society in the manor house just as much as Ella was. They became friends as Ella's understanding of the Scots language grew with no one the wiser.

With the fifth day without Callum looming on the morrow, Ella had just about given up hope. Plots about how to gain access to Duncan's bedchamber chest so she might search for the other charmstone crossed Ella's mind many times that day. But first, she had to find out where his room was, and where the stone was, and what if nothing happened when she touched the stones together?

Noticing a different pace in the kitchen, Ella raised her brows at Oswald again after pointing to the serving maids carving large slices of boar and goat meat onto platters.

"They are preparin' a cold repast for Sunday dinner," Oswald spoke slowly and pointed at items so Ella might follow what he was saying. "We dinnae stoke the fire on a Sunday. 'Tis forbidden." These were all words Ella knew. Placing her hands together to look like she was praying, Ella raised her brows again.

"Nay, the chaplain holds the service in the hall - the chapel cannae be used 'til the castle stairs are mended."

Ella nodded and smiled. She couldn't ask for a better or more patient teacher than the skinny boy sweating on the stool by the spit.

***

Although it was still dark the next morning when Callum shook her gently awake, Ella did not need the smoldering embers of the fire to know it was him. The captain was in her dreams, waking or sleeping, and she knew his touch and masculine scent as if they were her own.

He pressed his finger to her lips. Understanding this silent communication, Ella rose to get dressed, such as it was. She had learned to wrap her hair under the cap to hide it, using the long ribands to tighten the headgear so her hair was not showing; if it was, Oswald had taught Ella any red-blooded Middle Age man would have been well within his rights to take that as a sign that she wanted him to woo her.

But before she could hide her soft, silver hair, Callum lightly gripped her wrist to stop her. Their eyes locked and Ella felt her heart beat louder and faster. All he did was run his hand along her cheek, brushing it against her ear with a warming touch, and then spreading his fingers wide to comb her hair through with a sensual stroke. It was the most alluring sensation Ella had ever felt. The fire pit embers glowed as a reflection in the blackness of his pupils, which made Ella think of wolves prowling around a campfire. He smiled and stood up, allowing her to tuck her hair away out of sight.

Ella bundled the pile of rags she used as a pillow back in the chest in the servants' parlor and wrapped the earasaid around her waist and the fur cloak over her shoulders. Nodding to Callum to let him know she was ready they left the kitchens together, guided by the lighted torch in the wall sconce at the top of the steps. Once they were in the passage, Ella whispered to him in fragmented and very rudimentary Scots.

"Where we go?"

Callum had been removing the torch from the sconce, but this so surprised him that he spun around quickly, leaving a trail of fire in the air around him. "Where did ye learn that?"

Ella hushed him and he raised his eyes to the rafters by way of apology. "I did signs - Oswald the spit turn boy - he teach me."

Callum hugged her around the shoulders, whispering in her ear. "Ye speak most sweetly, lass." Ella grinned. "Sweet is a word I learn too - honey." She was pleased when she saw the lopsided grin on his face, but he spoke French back to her. "I will refine your pronunciation at a later date." He raised her hand and kissed it.

There was no more time for praise; Callum was propelling Ella down the passage at a fast pace after quietly telling her that they must go somewhere private to talk. Ella had given up trying to navigate the manor house at an early stage in her time transplant and Callum knew the passages and stairs so well he could walk them in the dark. They arrived at a quiet room, lined with wooden paneling, the scant furnishings pushed against the wall and out of the way.

"Where are we?" Ella whispered. The room was warm enough even though it held no fire grate. Callum did not answer her immediately; he lit two candles off the torch before dousing the flame in a bucket of water standing outside in the passage. After checking up and down the passage and listening carefully, he came back into the room.

"The cleric uses this chamber for prayer and confession," he told Ella, indicating an ornately carved armchair next to a side table on which a flagon of wine sat on a tray. After pulling a footstool closer to the chair, he sat down and patted the small stool for Ella to sit on.

"Come, lass. Dinnae be afeard. We must talk. I am here as my uncle's envoy."

She sat. Ella's heart was in her mouth. There was something about the composed way Callum was observing her that had echoed Sir Colin's calm acceptance of her arrival at his home.

"Ella…me uncle and I conversed for many hours after ye lost yer senses. We spoke until the candles guttered in the tallow catch. Would ye care to guess what he said?"

Had he brought her here for her confession? Could she trust him enough to tell him the truth?

"If ye were to press me, Callum, I would say Sir Colin has a better idea about where I am from than he let on when I was first presented to him?"

Callum sighed and nodded slowly as his suspicions were confirmed. "Aye, ye have that correct." He switched to French so she would understand everything he was saying to her. "Ella, my uncle believes that you had access to the other half of the family charmstone… and that you come from a place too far away for our comprehension. Can I tell you why he believes this?"

"Aye," she whispered, but the word seemed to echo around the wood-paneled walls.

"You have seen the amulet my cousin Duncan wears on his breast? Aye, as heir he has the right to bear the Campbell charmstone, but it was my uncle's first. He found the stone amidst the ruins of an ancient city's shrine in the sands of the south.

You must know that Lady Margaret is not Sir Colin's first wife. Before her was the Lady Marriot. The true Lady of Loch Awe. The bards tell of the great love Sir Colin and Lady Marriot had for one another. They were lovers contrary to the church's teaching; it is said they were beloved of one another from an early age, younger than my sister Margaret is now, for it was as if their love was destined.

"Now, here is where you must listen. Sir Colin told me he traveled back to Castle Kilchurn by an unorthodox method after finding the stone. He would not elaborate much more than that to me. When he returned to Lady Marriot, they were not able to touch one another for some time after because it pained them."

Callum stared intently at Ella. "I asked my uncle to describe the pain he felt whenever he touched Mariott. He said it was like a sharp ache that raised the hair of the skin and crackled like lightning - as if

Thor had thrown a lightning bolt into his heart. 'Twas the same for Lady Mariott. No one else suffered this effect."

Ella said nothing, just stared at the hem of her earasaid, pleating it into folds.

"Now, the first truth I must hear from you, Ella, is this? Did you scare off any brigands with the same trick? You told me when they touched you, the brigands were shaken with the same pain. Or did you only experience it with me?"

"Only you," Ella said in a soft voice. He seemed pleased with this answer, and so continued.

"After Lady Mariott's sad passing, my uncle was inconsolable. In a fit of grief and madness, he ordered for the charmstone to be cut in twain, keeping one half for himself and placing the other half in Lady Mariott's tomb. The stone was damaged during the cutting - separating too soon which caused one stone to dominate the other. My uncle kept the smaller half that was missing a wee piece on top; he left the dominant half of the stone with his Lady. After your arrival, Sir Colin caused his beloved wife's tombstone to be prised open.

"How do I know this? Because my uncle and I were the ones to do it. He was too distraught to search the tomb, so I was the one to report back to him that the charmstone amulet, that he had placed so lovingly in Mariott's last resting place, was gone." Again, Callum bent his head to watch her face as she answered him. "Did you take the stone? Do you know the person who robbed the Lady's grave?"

"Nay," Ella shuddered at the thought of doing such a thing.

That made him frown. "Sir Colin will nae believe that answer, Ella. He cannae be moved from the absolute conviction that ye touched Lady Mariott's half of the charmstone and it somehow brought ye here by unorthodox means."

After he repeated it in French, Ella's dilemma intensified. "What would ye have me say, Callum? If I say aye, the priest will say I have had dealings with the diabhal! If I say nay, I would be lying."

Standing up so quickly that his chair squeaked and teetered before rattling back down onto four legs, Callum began to stride about the room, raking his unruly red hair in frustration. "You will not say it? Very well, then I will because my uncle already knows."

Coming to a stop in front of Ella's stool, Callum fell down onto his knees in front of her. "Sweet Ella, my uncle believes that you arrived in our land by magick. Somehow, you gained access to the charmstone from whence it was taken from my late aunt's tomb, but when you touched it, the only power the Campbell amulet had was to bring you back to its true home."

He buried his head in her lap and Ella could not resist running her hands through his wild hair. His muffled voice said, "Ella, lass, all me uncle wants to know is where the other stone is." Callum raised his face to look at her. "And what do ye ken about the Knights of Khronos?"

Chapter 10

There was no way Ella was going to tell Callum about the charmstone hidden under her many layers of clothing, but she wanted to know more about the Knights of Khronos. None of her fairy tales growing up had mentioned such an organization.

"Why could Sir Colin not ask me these questions himself, Callum?" Ella hated feeling suspicious about the only person she trusted or cared for, but she could not shake the images of witches being burnt at the stake out of her mind.

Standing up slowly, Callum sat back in the chair to continue. "My uncle's household has fallen into two opposing camps, taking half the soldiers one way and half the other. It is a…difficult situation and requires much diplomacy: Sir Colin and Lady Margaret have fallen out over you. Lady Margaret is a powerful enemy to have at the best of times, but unfortunately my cousin Duncan has sided with her.

Ella's blood froze at his words and without knowing it, Ella shifted closer to Callum, placing a cold hand on the woolen hose he had on under his plaid, tucked into his boots. "Tell me what's going on, I beg ye, Callum."

He sighed, stretching out his long legs and crossing them. "Sir Colin simply sees ye as a young girl who somehow got to touch the stone and thus become its envoy for it to return back to the Lady of Loch Awe. The only ones who would be motivated to rob the tomb would be the Knights of Khronos."

"Who are they?"

"Sir Colin has had dealings with the Knights in the past. He did not tell me very much about them. But if they are Knights, then surely their motives are pure? My uncle will be disappointed to hear you do not have the stone, lass."

Seeing a way out of her dilemma and hoping she was choosing correctly to support Sir Colin, Ella took a deep breath and said, "Your uncle is right, Callum…I was far away and I grabbed hold of the other half of the charmstone…and it brought me here. But-but when I found myself in the water, I accidentally dropped the amulet in the loch."

She looked at him carefully to see if he could detect her deception, but Callum was too relieved to finally hear the truth to notice the signs. "If we were to return to Bonawe isle, lass, d'ye think we might be able to find the place again? The tides go out half a league or more at certain times of the moon cycle. Surely ye can mark the spot!" Callum was beginning to come alive with enthusiasm again. "I'll take ten or twelve strong men with us to dig up the sand."

That was when Ella began to realize how important the matching charmstone was to Sir Colin. Not only had he smashed a magical artifact so that his wife could be buried with it, but he was prepared to alienate half his household and his wife and son to get it back. Sending Callum as his intermediary was a way to dodge the close scrutiny Sir Colin must be under.

"Wait," she placed a restraining hand on his arm. "Am I - are we in any danger from this? Is Duncan a formidable foe?"

Holding Ella in his arms, Callum lifted her chin up with one hand and smiled down at her. "Ye ask questions like a man, lass," she could feel that rumble of laughter in his chest, "would I be doin' this if it was dangerous for ye? As long as I'm around, Duncan cannae harm ye. Aye, he has a poisonous tongue which could cause a wee bit o' mischief, but he's too much of a backbiter to come at me head-on."

Ella had to agree with him. How dangerous could a man be if he chose to wear shoes that looked like wedges of melting cheese? But Callum was not finished warning her yet. "Until I muster the men, ye must stay in the kitchen, out of sight of Lady Margaret and Duncan. Albeit the Lady wants ye gone from here because she mistrusts yer bonny face, but Duncan wants ye in his bed."

Stifling a giggle, Ella shook her head. "No way," she said in English, and then managed to change it to sound like 'nay'.

His embrace tightened around her. "D'ye say that because yer heart has turned to another, Ella?"

The candlelight, the warm paneled chamber, and even the painted triptych wood panels showing images of saints staring out from the flat surface made Ella more aware of the blood pumping in her face, her chest, and the lower parts of her stomach. She did not need a sign-post to tell her this was love.

"Me heart has turned to ye, Captain," Ella was too shy to look up at him, and buried her face in his chest after saying it. He stroked her head and neck gently,

"It heals me heart to hear ye say that, lass," Callum said in his deep voice, "because I have loved ye from the start. My uncle knows this and approves the match…but we have many tasks ahead of us before we can enjoy our love in leisure."

The thought of being at leisure to lie in bed with Callum and show him how deeply she loved him was very tempting to Ella. "How soon can we leave and sail back to the isle?" she asked him. Callum bent to place a chaste kiss on her lips. "Promise me that ye will wait patiently for me in the kitchens until the morrow? We will leave at dawn - eight bells after midnight."

She promised him, and they spent a few precious moments doing what every young couple in love did before parting for a brief while. Those few precious moments were all it took for Ella to know that she wanted to live with Callum for the rest of her life. All of the cynical disbelief she had experienced after reading about such things happening in the real world was replaced by astonishment that it was now happening to her. Ella felt the twenty-first century fading slowly away.

She would pretend to find the charmstone and return it to Sir Colin so that Callum and she could get married. That was all Ella wanted from her new life now.

**

She was waiting for him at dawn. When Callum ducked his head under the door lintel in the kitchen, Ella gave Oswald a kiss farewell, keeping up her act as mute and hard of hearing to the end.

Callum kissed her once they were out of sight of any servants, but he was in a rush to ride to Loch Awe. "Duncan has been alerted to our activity," he told Ella curtly after tossing her onto the saddle side-ways, "we must leave before he manages to rile his men up to act out his orders."

Ella clung on for dear life as the captain kicked his horse into a wild canter. With her mouth smothered against his cuirass to hide her face from the cold, Ella managed to scream into the wind. "What will he do? He cannae go against yer uncle's orders!"

"He has mentioned the need for us to wait for the priest. It is a reasonable enough request. Perhaps, like us, Lady Margaret and Duncan walk with one foot in the shadows."

They had arrived at the loch. The castle was already a hive of activity, with craftsmen erecting a massive tread stone and stonemasons grinding rocks with a thick mixture of silt and water on a copper saw.

Only one longboat was waiting for them, and only four soldiers were in the hull. Callum looked too grim for her to ask questions, but Ella felt a swell of fear. She hesitated. "I will carry ye o'er the water, lass," Callum reassured her. "Dinnae fash aboot vittles either - I have plenty enough in the boat."

Ella shook her head. "I must have taken too long a pull at the small beer, Callum. Might I dash into the copse to relieve meself afore we embark?"

He gave her that devastatingly gorgeous grin of his again. "Och, was that the reason for yer consternation, lass? Go on wi' ye then!"

They both laughed as Ella ran to the copse, hitching up her tunic as she reached the perimeter.

She never even got to squat down. Running to move out of sight in the thicket of bushes, Ella ran straight into a group of soldiers hiding amongst the trees. Before she could scream, a calloused hand covered her mouth and her legs were kicked out underneath her.

"What good fortune," Duncan's oily voice came from behind the soldier's head. Still muffling her mouth with his hand, Duncan gestured for the soldier to remove it. "Ye will nae require a hand, lad, if ye use one o' these." Duncan casually removed a dirk from the pouch around his belt and passed it to the soldier, who promptly pressed the sharp tip against the jugular vein in Ella's neck.

She stopped struggling and went silent. "That's better," Duncan said serenely, "Now hold her down and spread her legs for me. I want a go on this white mare before me winsome cousin has her."

The soldiers did as they were told, one pressing the dirk against her throat and another two pulling her legs open. "One squawk and you're dead, wench," Duncan hissed. Pulling his codpiece flap down so he could bring himself up to face the task.

Ella retched and tried to turn her face to the side so she would not have to swallow her bile, but the dirk stopped her. This could not be happening. This was not the way her beautiful Highland romance was meant to end…and it would end if this man touched her in the way he was planning to because Ella knew she would scream.

Goodbye, Callum, my love, my handsome, braw, Scottish warrior. Avenge my death if it eases your pain, but only if it doesn't cause you harm.

Duncan was ready and primed. He lay down on top of her, tearing her shift and tunic open to expose her breasts. He tried to kiss her…

The charmstones connected.

Everything around Ella went black. She was falling. There was no pain except in her heart because she knew she was moving away from Captain Callum Campbell - the only man she would ever love.

A NOTE FROM THE AUTHOR

Thank you for reading Enchanted By The Highlander. Please consider leaving a review so others can know if you enjoyed the book.

Book two will take you from Ella's initial arrival and experiences in 1452 Scotland, back to modern Scotland and then to 1453 where her adventures with her love Callum take more exciting twists.

'He kissed her, and that was all the touch Ella needed to know that she belonged to Callum in every single way.'

A young couple with a love and passion for one another that neither time nor space can hold. But this time, different players have joined the game, and they are lethally dangerous and endowed with more than just magic.

Back in modern Scotland, Ella Campbell's return causes a riot. But once the police have washed their hands of the strange blond-haired tourist and her stranger stories, Ella is free to find her way back to Medieval times—and to Callum, her braw, dark Highland warrior.

The Scottish coastal Highlands in 1453 is not a good time and place to present as a witch, and Callum is not the only man waiting impatiently for Ella's return. There's Father Archibald, the Loch Awe priest, and now Duncan Campbell, the Campbell son and heir, who have joined forces with those who think love and passion are black magic enough without adding time travel to the equation!

Will Ella survive the twisted fate mapped out for her? Or will time snatch her away from the love of her life once more?

Please enjoy Book Two in The Lady of Loch Awe Scottish Time-Traveling Historical romance novel.

Available on Amazon
Making Magic With The Highlander
By Kalani Madden

https://mybook.to/LadyOfLochAweBk2

GET YOUR FREE BOOK

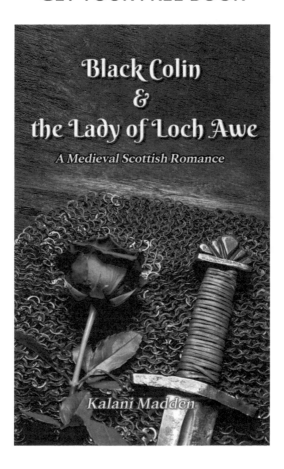

Use this link directly in your browser.
https://dl.bookfunnel.com/uneo04po50

Who was the first Lady of Loch Awe and why is she so important? Please enjoy this FREE book and origin story about a passionate love that will not listen to the boundaries of space and time.A young couple with a love and passion for one another that neither time nor space can hold. But this time, different players have joined the game, and they are lethally dangerous and endowed with more than just magic.

Sir Colin Campbell is a Knight and Crusader in the prime of his life. The villagers at Glenurchy call him the Wolf Cub and his vassals call him Black Col because of his dark hair.

Colin's heart belonged to Maiden Mariott from the first time they met and she could not take her eyes off her tall, dark, and mysteriously handsome suitor.

But true love does not always run smoothly. The Black Knight is called away on another Crusade after Baron MacCorquodale decides he wants Lady Mariott for himself.

Things look bleak until the Black Knight finds a lost relic that would change the course of his life forever…as it would also change the lives of every Campbell son who came into contact with the relic too.

Based on the Myth and Legend of Black Colin Campbell, a true Scottish Hero.

Kalani Madden wrote this FREE book especially for all fans of epic time travel Scottish historical romance. Enjoy.

Made in United States
Troutdale, OR
06/09/2023

10527295R10060